the place between breaths

Also by An Na

The Fold
A Step from Heaven
Wait for Me

the place between breaths

an na

A̶ A Caitlyn Dlouhy Book
atheneum

New York   London   Toronto   Sydney   New Delhi

atheneum

An imprint of Simon & Schuster Children's Publishing Division
1230 Avenue of the Americas, New York, New York 10020
This book is a work of fiction. Any references to historical events, real people, or real places are used fictitiously. Other names, characters, places, and events are products of the author's imagination, and any resemblance to actual events or places or persons, living or dead, is entirely coincidental.
Text copyright © 2018 by An Na
Jacket illustration copyright © 2018 by Levente Szabo
All rights reserved, including the right of reproduction in whole or in part in any form.
Atheneum logo is a trademark of Simon & Schuster, Inc.
For information about special discounts for bulk purchases, please contact Simon & Schuster Special Sales at 1-866-506-1949 or business@simonandschuster.com.
The Simon & Schuster Speakers Bureau can bring authors to your live event. For more information or to book an event, contact the Simon & Schuster Speakers Bureau at 1-866-248-3049 or visit our website at www.simonspeakers.com.
Book design by Debra Sfetsios-Conover and Irene Metaxatos
The text for this book was set in Bembo Std.
Manufactured in the United States of America
First Edition
10 9 8 7 6 5 4 3 2 1
CIP data for this book is available from the Library of Congress.
ISBN 978-1-4814-2225-3 (hc)
ISBN 978-1-4814-2227-7 (eBook)

With gratitude and love for my sisters:
Jin, Jacqueline, and Juliet

Life begins on the other side of despair.

—JEAN PAUL SARTRE

Winter SpringSummerAutumn

There are many versions of a story. Many sides and lenses that can distort, change, illuminate what is seen and unseen. What is heard and unheard. What is felt and unfelt. In the end, truth is but a facet of a diamond, a spark of ray from the sun, a forget-me-not flower seen from the eyes of a bee. What lives and breathes as reality is a perception, so who is to say what is possible and impossible?

Call it fate or simply coincidence, but the shorter version of how I found you begins like this. There was a dark speck on the side of the barren winter road that grew larger and larger as I drove closer. Expanding from a dot to a stone to a tree stump until I screeched to a halt. A few dozen feet away from a headless coat turtle-shelled on top of the snow. Both of my hands released the steering wheel and coned over my mouth. Was it a body? There was no movement. I slowly opened the door and stepped out. Had someone frozen and died overnight? It wouldn't have been the first time that something like that happened around here. I took a step forward, and then another, the fragile crack of ice and gravel rippling through me. My breath misted before my face.

A head emerged.

I shouted in fright. "You scared the hell out of me!" A large vapor cloud formed as I exhaled long and slow.

Your disheveled black hair framed your face, petite, round. It was hard to tell how old you were, but something about your eyes told me you were older than you looked.

Slowly unfurling each limb as though in pain, you stood up.

I walked forward in relief.

"You looked like a dead body."

Your brows gathered as you lifted and dropped your shoulders before bowing your head slightly. "Sorry."

Then a brief wave of your hand and you started walking down the side of the road.

"Do you need a ride?" I called to your back. You stopped. "I'm on my way to town," I said.

You gazed back, your eyes roaming my face before you turned and kept walking down the long cold road. Away from me.

∘ ∘ ∘

That is the short version of how we met. You didn't tell me then why you were so tired that you had to rest hiding inside your coat by the side of the road, but since then, after meeting again, you have shared a few of your truths. The longer story of us is like the horizon. We can only know what we see, and all that we wish we could understand is beyond vision.

Winter Spring SummerAutum

The alarm beats relentlessly into my mind and I choke for air, ragged heaves pushing in and out as though I have been underwater far too long. My hand moves swiftly to turn off the incessant noise. The soft morning light flickers into my eyes before I close them again. The fading remnants of my dream, my mother's face, haunt me. They come and go like spring rains, sometimes light and steady, sometimes fleeting mist, and then the occasional, torrential downpour. Her profile lights my mind. The dark line of her eyebrow. The labyrinth swirls of her ear. The gentle round of her nose and the sharp blade of her jawline.

In my worst moments, I wish her dead. At least then

I could truly mourn. But to be missing for such a long time without any sign, lost or dead, just a name in the police data bank . . . The yearning for clarity sifts through me until all that lingers is the cancer of uncertainty. I have only the briefest memories, and these dreams, to tell me that she even existed at all. I glance over at the clock and finally force myself out of bed. The routine for school, if nothing else, is comforting in its predictability.

In the kitchen, I make the coffee and pour two cups. Cradling my hot mug, I check the outdoor thermometer from the window above the sink. Fourteen degrees. It has got to warm up any day now. I have said this for the last two weeks and the average temperature still hovers at twenty. The wind rattles the window above the sink.

"Nineteen."

I turn around and find Dad standing in the doorway, dressed for work.

"Close," I say. "Fourteen."

Dad throws his blue tie over one shoulder and walks to the counter for his coffee and his laptop.

"You look tired this morning, Grace." Dad tips his head to the side as he stares into my face. I lower my eyes and turn away from his hawk gaze.

"Just dreams, Dad," I say lightly. "And I have midterms coming up."

I can feel his focus shifting away, since he's satisfied with my answer.

"Maybe you should cut back on some hours at the lab, Gracie."

I don't bother to respond. The internship at Genentium is coveted by high schoolers looking for a way into the best colleges. I know that the other interns and doctors there think I landed a spot because of Dad, who works on the corporate end, and that means constantly proving I belong. But Dad doesn't understand or maybe doesn't care. He is too busy already at his computer, buried in the database of the National Missing and Unidentified Persons Systems site, checking his e-mails, his science journals online.

His winter pallor makes him look tired too, though most people couldn't tell you if he had a tan or not because of his darker complexion. For a white man, that is. But then who can say if he really is white? With his olive skin tone and coarse black curly hair, he could be part black or Southeast Asian or Native American or Latino or Mediterranean. We joke and change his ethnicity based on the restaurant we are eating in. Dad was adopted and has never attempted to locate his birth parents. An irony not lost to someone who lives and breathes for genetics. I've tried to get him to take a DNA test, but he says he likes being a chameleon. The genetic history that he cares about the most is not his, but hers. And there was never any doubt of her Korean heritage or the disease that destroyed her. My mother's bloodline, after all, is mine.

By trade, Dad is a headhunter for one of the most

prestigious labs in the country. The world. It is his job to know the research, the routines, the likes and dislikes of the top scientists in the field of genetics. It is his job to lure them away from where they are to come and work for Genentium.

By heart, Dad is looking for a miracle. It is not a coincidence that he came to work for this lab. We moved here specifically, strategically, so he would have the funding, the power, and the reputation to entice the best scientists in the world to work on the research and treatment for genetic diseases like sickle cell anemia, Parkinson's, cancer, Huntington's, schizophrenia. Dad never talks about cures, only speaks about the research and the scientists making discoveries every day. But I know what he wants. I know like I know without a doubt that I am his daughter. We are looking for a cure. It is a race he and I lost long ago, the moment my mother's schizophrenia overtook her again, forcing her to step out of the house one last time. But that doesn't stop Dad from still crawling to the finish line, hope lashed to his back. He waits for her to return, to be found. And finally, finally, their love, our family, whole again, just as they had always dreamed.

I open a drawer and pull out a spoon. Dad is unaware of my movements. He is already on the hunt.

"So who are you trying to recruit next?" I ask, and walk to the refrigerator to get some yogurt.

Dad holds up one finger and then types quickly.

I take my yogurt to the small table in the corner of

the kitchen, where the latest journal of *Nature* sits waiting for me.

"Dr. Samuels."

"Isn't he a little young?" I ask, digging into my yogurt. I've heard Dad talking about Samuels. He's some hotshot wunderkind scientist from San Diego's Scripps Research Institute. Supposedly, he already has three patents to his name, and that was before he even got out of graduate school. I wonder how Dr. Mendelson would get along with him. She doesn't like a lot of bullshit in her lab. She barely tolerates the interns, but she knows it's good for community building and fostering young minds, or so she says at the awards ceremony and press junkets. Twenty different questions spring to mind, but now is not the right time. I'll talk to Dad later, when his eyes aren't glued to the screen. Besides, he won't talk about it in the morning. Not when his mind is fresh and ready to tackle the next set of problems. It's in the evening, when he is tired and has a beer in hand, that talking about the possibilities doesn't sound so reckless, like playing the lottery with the last dollar in your pocket.

Dad runs his hands over his eyes as though resetting his vision.

"Are you okay, Dad?"

"Just got dizzy for a second." Dad waves away my concern. Doctors are the worst patients. Even though he traded in his ER scrubs for a suit and tie, he's still a stubborn doctor under all that dress-up. I remember the exact moment he stopped going into the hospital; it was a month after Mama had disappeared. He was reading an article about the discovery of the Huntington's gene. He looked up and said to me, "*I can't find a cure, but I can find the scientists who will.*"

He traded in medicine for research, practice for reading scientific journals and analyzing spreadsheets and interviews of geneticists. There was only so much a single doctor could do, but an entire orchestra of scientists working together, that was real progress. After moving here for Genentium, however, work has spiked a fever. Sometimes I barely see him, since he is either traveling or working late.

I push away my half-eaten yogurt, my appetite suddenly gone, and pick up my mug. As I sip my coffee, I stare at the bowl of fruit at the center of the table. The pears are pale with faint brown spotting. I reach out and press. The point at which ripeness crosses over into decay is unperceivable. Only the fact remains. The slight overly sweet, acrid stench. The soft yielding flesh. The discoloration. I pick up the bowl and throw the entire contents into the trash.

At the front door, I grab my backpack off the coat hook and yell back, "Bye, Dad. I'll see you after work."

"Bye, bugaboo."

I know he hasn't even looked up from the screen.

As soon as I step outside, the frost slaps my face, making me gasp for air. I'm so done with this cold I want to scream. Instead I take out my anger on the steps and stomp down. At the bottom, as I move past the shadow of the house into the sun, a patch of colors catches my eyes. The first gladiators of spring wave their blue and yellow flags against the snow. Family: Iridaceae. Genus: *Crocus*. Legend: the symbol of the Greek noble Crocus's undying love for the nymph Smilax.

I sigh and walk over to them. Crouching low, I touch the fragile blossoms. Time expands and contracts, boundless, but always forward. Only the seasons remind me of what has passed and what is to come. I can't believe it's been almost a year since we moved here to Jericho because it was close enough to the lab in Chicago. Since Dad and I first drove out to see the house, the lines of the building emerging from the field like a kindergarten drawing. The miles of green swaying grass, the white turret with wide encircling porch, pretty as a lady flouncing her skirts. I knew Dad had made up his mind before we had even stepped inside. He got out of the car and immediately bent down to pick the tiny periwinkle blossoms surrounding the front steps, interwoven into the lawn and gardens. The house sat in the middle of a field of forget-me-nots. Family: Boraginaceae. Genus: *Myosotis*. Legend: my mother's favorite flower.

It still kills me that Dad wanted to live so far away from anyone or any place. It takes us at least forty minutes to get anywhere: school, the city, the lab. Luckily, we still have Mom's car, which became mine as soon as I learned to drive. The black Lincoln Continental moves like a boat in a storm, but Dad won't hear of replacing it. It's solid. Built to last, Dad likes to joke, with that lopsided grin that always makes him look like the used car salesman he once was when he was my age. Still, a car is a car, and without this boat, I would never be able to leave the house. I would be a captive in the tower forever.

I pat the hood, silently greeting my car, and step inside. With both hands firmly on the steering wheel, I drive out onto the desolate frozen road. Any sudden jerk can throw the entire thing into a tailspin. A rut or bump can mean sitting by the side of the road for hours before someone stops to lend a hand. I drive carefully over the snowblown roads. A few miles from school, I spot Hannah standing in her usual spot.

"Hey," she says as she steps into the car and immediately places her hands over the heating vent. "I damn near froze my ass off last night."

I slowly ease back onto the dirt road and keep my eyes peeled for any bumps.

"Why won't this winter end? We're low on wood," Hannah complains.

"It can't stay cold forever," I respond. "I mean, it's March; spring must be right around the corner."

Hannah smiles. "You sound like Frog."

I glance over at her, raise one eyebrow.

Hannah baps me on the shoulder. "God, were you raised by wolves? For such a geek, I can't believe how little you've read. Frog and Toad. Remember reading Frog and Toad back in, like, second grade or something?"

I shrug. My memories are not always reliable.

"It's the one good thing my mom did before she cut out," Hannah says. "But you were probably reading *National Geographic* instead of having a normal childhood."

I snort. "If normal means moving all the time so that you're so far behind in school you have the great distinction of being the oldest kid in high school, yeah sure, it was super normal."

"Shut up, you're not the oldest. I thought Andy Deter was the oldest."

We drive over a bump and I grip the steering wheel harder. "Nope," I say through clenched teeth. "I beat him by six months, easy."

Hannah reaches over and touches my hair. "Yup, it's gray. Okay, Granny, you win."

I swat her hand away and Hannah laughs, leaning back into the seat and digging around in her jacket pocket before pulling out sections of granola bar from a foil wrapper. She pops one into her mouth. Soon a crinkling and smacking noise, like a small ravenous animal, fills the car. Hannah worries the wrapper in her hands as she stares out her window. Her sudden silence tugs at me.

"Tell me a Frog and Toad story," I say.

She keeps her gaze toward her window but responds faintly, "Frog and Toad are best friends, and they have all these adventures together."

"Really? Frogs and toads prefer different habitats."

Hannah laughs, spraying bits of granola all over the dashboard. "You are such a nerd."

I accept this honor with a beauty-queen wave.

Hannah smashes the wrapper in her hands and balls it up before shoving it into her coat pocket. She turns and tucks herself deep into her seat. "Well, my favorite one was about the time Frog wanted to be alone, and Toad starts freaking out because he thinks his friend doesn't like him anymore."

"That sounds terrible. Why's that your favorite?"

"Just listen." Hannah draws her knees up to her chest. "Frog wanted to be alone to think about all the wonderful things in his life. The sun shining, how being a frog was so great, and having the best friend in the world, Toad. But Toad, who's kind of insecure and always jumping to the worst thoughts, thinks that Frog is mad at him and doesn't want to be his friend anymore."

"So Frog's the optimist and Toad's the pessimist?"

"Sort of."

"Like yin and yang."

"Or two sides of a coin."

"So what happens in the end?"

"Toad makes some sandwiches and iced tea and tries to take them out to Frog, who's sitting on a rock in the lake, thinking his happy thoughts. But as Toad's on his way out there, he falls and everything ends up in the water."

"No wonder he's a pessimist."

Hannah snaps her fingers and points at me. "But Frog doesn't care and tells Toad he's a great friend anyway and they eat the wet sandwiches sitting on the rock together. The end."

"I would say eating cold, wet sandwiches is truly a testament to friendship and love."

"I would eat wet sandwiches with you," Hannah says softly.

I keep my eyes on the road and smile. "Me too."

Before long the town's buildings appear on the horizon. Hannah's arms wrap around her middle as though she is cold.

"Do you want me to turn up the heat?" I ask.

"No, I'm fine." Hannah's expression hardens as she spies at the gray buildings ahead. I stop at a red light.

"You okay?"

Hannah's eyes suddenly glisten with pooling tears. "Shit," she says.

"Whoa, wait, what's up?" The light turns green and I speed over to the side of the road. "Hannah, what's wrong?"

Hannah covers her face with her hands.

"Come on, Frog and Toad, right?"

She nods, but her hands do not drop.

"Tell me."

"I'm pregnant."

"Oh, Hannah!" I reach over and gently pull down her hands. Tears stream down her cheeks.

"Are you sure?" I feel the trembling in her bones.

She nods.

"Oh man. Or should I say, oh Dave."

"Stop." She pulls her hands from mine and rubs away the tears with her fingers.

"I just . . . I just didn't think things were that serious with you two. I thought it was strictly messing around."

Hannah glares at me. "God, for a fucking scientist, you know nothing about biology."

"I study genetics, not physiology."

"Grace, you're not helping."

"Sorry, sorry." I take a deep breath. "So . . . how long . . . never mind. So what are you going to do? Are you going to tell him?"

Hannah chews her lower lip but doesn't answer.

"This is heavy. Like Lifetime movie after-school special heavy," I try to joke.

Hannah looks like she is going to cry again.

I hold up my hands. "Wait, wait. It's going to be okay, Hannah. We are going to get through this. I'm your Frog or your Toad. Who's the optimist again? Whichever it is, I'm your amphibian."

I can see Hannah beginning to smile as I shift out of park. We silently drive through town until we reach the high school. The concrete buildings jut out in odd places, additions tacked on over the years as this part of the small farm community grew into a suburb to the city. Mounds of dirty snow lie scattered along the outskirts of the school.

There are a few bare patches of gray-green frozen lawn exposed near the buildings of this holding pen they call high school. Small groups of kids stand on the sidewalk talking, huddled together against the cold.

Hannah stiffens as she scans the crowd. I press on the gas and try to pass the groups as quickly as possible in case Dave Ridley happens to be in one of them. Once we are on the far side of the parking lot, Hannah slowly uncurls from her seat. She leans forward, resting her forearms on the dashboard.

"I can't go in there," she says. "I don't want to bump into him."

"Just ignore him."

Hannah stares at me. "Just pretend I'm not pregnant? I don't know how not to be pregnant, Grace. I have a baby growing inside me."

"It's not really a baby. It's a zygote."

"Do you always have to be the scientist?"

"I can't help the way my mind works." I shrug. "You know you have choices, right, Hannah?"

"I know," she says, her voice hollow. "But so does he."

"What does that mean?"

She twists her mouth to one side. "I mean, what if he wants to keep it?"

I stare at her incredulously. Does she really believe Dave wants to have a baby with her?

Hannah refuses to look up. She has the granola bar wrapper out. "He said he loves me."

"He loves you," I repeat. Love. It is an emotion like no other. Wars, murder, heroic deeds, sacrifice, suffering, all in the name of love. What is it to know this kind of love?

I study myself in the rearview mirror. My eyes so much like hers. The slope of my cheekbones. The curving upper bow of my lips. Hers. But the rest of me, the small moles marking secret places on the body, the freckles across my nose and cheeks, the way I walk—feet slightly pigeon-toed—that is my father. In me lives everything that my parents hoped and dreamed for all those years they were alone and dreamed of finding a love singular and true. I remember the way they looked at each other. Like thread and needle, each useless without the other. Dave Riley has never looked at Hannah that way. How do you tell your friend that he probably doesn't love you enough to have a child with you? To marry you?

"Your mom and dad did it," Hannah says, her eyes pleading with me to agree. "They had you when your mom was nineteen, you said. It was the love story your father had always dreamed about."

"Yeah, but . . . that was different."

"How? How is that different for your parents and not for me?"

I look away from her. How do you tell someone the truth? "Dad really loved Mom."

I hear the click of her seat belt. The car door slams and she is gone.

o o o

From my peripheral vision, I catch glimpses of Hannah throughout the day, but she disappears behind bodies and corners each time I approach. At lunch I sit by myself at one of the tables in the back, waiting and hoping Hannah has forgiven me. Waves of people move through the cafeteria, but Hannah is not one of them. I gaze down at my fries and grilled cheese, and the heavy, greasy odor begins to choke my senses. I push the tray away, but relief will not come. Instead I can feel the warmth, the pulsing heartbeats of all the people around me, a fine mist of sweat and breath mingling together and coating my skin like a slick layer of oil. I stand up and leave my tray on the table, rushing for the double doors. Shoving my hip hard against the horizontal metal bar, I push open the door and run out into the hallway.

In the distance half a dozen kids walk toward me. I catch sight of Dave in the pack. The way Dave jostles into his friend, leaning in to say something private as he points to the girl walking in front of him, makes me sick. Hannah has said over and over that Dave is a really good guy. Sweet, even. But everything I've observed and noted does not support that conclusion. In fact, I would say the exact opposite. He is a pig and Hannah would be so much better off without him. Dave looks up and catches me staring at him. He lifts his chin at me in recognition. I quickly turn and head down the hall toward my next class, journalism, which is really just working on the school newspaper and the yearbook.

Everyone is already at the conference table, looking over a few of the full-page spreads. I'm in no mood to talk or listen, so I head over to a computer and pull up the photo account to see what new pictures have been posted. Ashley Pines has posted a bunch of selfies of her and the cheerleading squad at the all-you-can-eat burger fund-raising night at Fuddruckers. There are a few good ones that I save of the whole group and one of Ashley chowing down on a burger, and I delete the rest. There are also a bunch of photos and selfies from the Academic Decathlon. They actually placed first in the state. I save a few of them standing with their trophy and delete the ones where they are partying like crazy.

"Hey, King," Justin shouts from across the room. "Did you finish the spread of Enchanted Sea Night?"

I sit back in my chair and crane my neck to see Justin. "It should be there. I uploaded it a few days ago."

"I didn't see it posted. Can you check it? Maybe the server crashed before it finished." I watch Justin go back to flirting with Amber, who is the senior quotes editor. Their blond heads merge together like a shampoo commercial. I would say they would have perfectly towheaded children except that I saw Amber's roots when we were working together on the senior portraits page. Luckily for them, if they want to have blond kids, they just have to insert a blond-generating SNP, otherwise known as a single-nucleotide polymorphism, a regulatory gene for hair color, into their embryo. Ahhh, genetics. It's like magic, but real.

I return to the photo account and save a few more pictures of the track team and the girls' lacrosse team before I switch platforms and look for the Enchanted Sea Night spread. Damn, it *did* crash before completely uploading. I hit upload again and watch the bar slowly crawl across the top of the page. The upload will take a while. I notice a small photo of Dave Riley in the corner, but he is with another girl whose face is turned away from the camera. He is smiling so wide you can see both rows of teeth. Could he really love Hannah? For her sake, I want it to be true. I want it so bad, I am even willing to stop the upload and go back in to Photoshop the black-haired girl out of the frame. There. At least Hannah won't see that he went with someone else to that stupid dance. I hit render and watch the new reality take form.

After school, I pace outside next to the administration building, waiting to see if Hannah will show up so I can give her a lift to her usual drop-off spot. As the minutes gather with no sign of her, the realization dawns. She is not coming. And I'm not surprised—why would she want someone like me as her friend? Who am I to tell Hannah that Dave doesn't love her? That he probably just used her for sex. What do I know about falling in . . . love? Dad ruined his whole life for love. An entire lifetime wasted on someone who was never going to come back. And if by some great miracle she did return, what would she have to offer him? Or me? Her love? Or just a life spent in a drug haze, moving from hospital to hospital like the first time?

Love is a word. A four-letter word that means nothing and everything to the wrong people. I start kicking at a bush by the sidewalk, thinking about all the times Dad made us move in the name of love. Most times I never even had a chance to make a friend before we were packing and leaving again. All for another lead at another lab. Another possible discovery. To help HER. I kick hard at the shrub and then reach down, begin yanking and pulling at the leaves. They scatter and fall to the ground. My anger and frustration pour out as I destroy this living thing until a calm begins to settle over me.

"Nice gardening work!"

There is a group of guys laughing and staring at me. Their eyes pass over my face, my body, their gaze like a physical presence of their judgment. My palms are streaked with green stains. I rub them on the sides of my jeans and walk quickly to my car. I can still see, from the corner of my eye, the group laughing. I jump into my car and gun it, screeching out of the parking lot. Rounding the corner, my front wheel hits the curb and my ribs smash into the steering wheel. The last ball of anger deflates in one motion as I pull over and clutch my side, panting.

The image of the group snickering at me plays over and over in my mind. Stupid. Idiot. Their mockery echoes loudly in my ears. I lean back against the headrest, massaging the knot on my rib cage that will show black and blue by tonight. A truck passes and I glance over. Was that

Hannah in the passenger seat? The misty silver of Dave's truck turns the corner and disappears.

Holding my breath, I try to make everything fade away: the pain in my ribs, the stench of school, Hannah, Dave, the leers, the green stains under my nails, Dad's irrepressible hope—I just need everything to stop for a minute. The swirling images and whispers gnaw at me until I am dizzy. The bright afternoon light streams in through the windshield. Pressing my fingertips hard to my temples, I close my eyes and force my mind to quiet. The sun presses against my closed lids, turning my world red.

WinterSpring **Summer** Autumn

The sun will beat against the closed lids of your eyes. Pools of blood will swim in your vision. You will believe for a moment that you are lying on a beach. Warm air blowing lightly across your face. A hand reaching over to cup the roundness of your shoulder as the voice murmurs, *Don't fall asleep. You'll burn.*

You will open your eyes, but the person is gone. Who? You search and search for the name, but the whispers crowd into your ears, erasing all your memories.

They will find you. They will find the shell of you lying on the street. You will try to tell them you are just sleeping, but there will be no sound. Your throat parched shut. You will watch them move around you, their lips like fish in speech. Though the sounds once familiar are now nothing, just wind speaking through trees, you will try to understand what they are saying. They pluck at your skin. Your clothes.

You will struggle away from them. Crouch down and hold your hands over your ears, but the voices are not outside. Are they? Are they, you stupid fuck? Stand up. Get up. Worthless. You're better off dead. Coward. Who do you think you are?

You will begin to cry. What do they want? You will begin to scream.

The warm breeze lifts the trash around you, blowing leaves, bits of torn paper, raising ghosts from the streets. The birds circle above, floating on the currents, dark shadows piercing sunlight. The red and blue lights flashing in your eyes, the men in black hats, the patch of gold on their dark shirts reflecting glints of light into your eyes. Until they close and roll back. The darkness will lift your body into the air. A weightless burden carried up up up on the rip-tides of grief like a particle of dust in a tornado.

Vinter Spring SummerAutumn

Large flakes of snow swirl and drift all around me as I step out of my car in the parking lot of Genentium. Above me the brilliant azure sky dots with white flakes. I marvel at the sight, opening my mouth to taste the blue that flits down on my face. Cold and clean, of light and air, I want to stand here all day in the perfection of this moment. I feel myself lifting into the sky. If I died right now, I would be happy. Forever.

But too swiftly, the sky grays over with clouds, the blueness disappearing, and the fading light dulling my vision. I lower my eyes and turn toward the building in which I will spend the rest of my afternoon. From the outside, Genentium looks like a bank consisting of sheer walls of glass on three sides. A waiting area with lounge chairs, a couch, a receptionist sitting behind a high counter, and a few security guards loitering around to finish off the resemblance. In reality, Genentium is a bunker filled with scientist bees working toward a common goal led by a queen, Dr. Mendelson. With each step toward Genentium, the idea of work tames my mind and I feel a part of a larger organism that tethers my body. I step inside the aquarium building and wave to Connie, the stooped-back receptionist, as I show security my badge.

On the elevator down to my lab, the doors open on B4, the animal floor. A guy with a tan too dark to be real for this part of the world pushes in a cart loaded with small compartments holding rats, two, sometimes three, per cage. I glance down at the rodents climbing up against the bars and sniffing the air. A few begin to squeak loudly. The elevator doors close and I find myself facing the guy with the fake tan. He briefly flashes me a smile before turning his attention to the squealing rats on the lower shelf of his cart. The noise is getting louder and louder. I stare at the numbers lighting up as we pass the floors. Why does my lab have to be on the lowest floor? The odor in the elevator is getting unbearable, not to mention the noise. The tan guy keeps checking the rats and then glancing up at me as though I am somehow responsible for their craziness. I start breathing through my mouth. I am just about to ask the guy what is wrong with them when the elevator doors open and he steps out backward. He easily swings the cart around and heads down the empty hallway. The fluorescent lighting turns the skin on the back of his neck a tropical orange. A slight screeching noise from a wheel is the only noise emanating from the cart now; the rats have suddenly become silent. The elevator closes.

On my floor, all the labs are hidden behind heavy metal doors. From the hallway, it's hard to imagine that there are close to a hundred scientists, lab techs, and assistants scurrying around the building. I remember my first day when Dr. Diaz, the supervising scientist for all the interns, gave us a guided tour as she introduced us to the various lab teams working on finding microscopic mutations—an extra gene sequence on some chromosome—chasing after a genetic history to different illnesses with a hereditary factor like breast cancer, diabetes, heart disease, depression. They were all down there searching for the clues that would lead to a discovery, and the hope for a cure, or at the very least, medication designed to target that specific condition. What Dr. Diaz didn't say, but Dad made clear as soon as he started working for Genentium, was that there was a shitload of money in patents to be made. Money that funded all the doctors that Dad could lure with abandon to work on what he wanted most—our family again.

I open the door to my lab and nod at some of the scientists standing at their stations. In a small room off to the side, I stow my gear on some shelves and change into my lab coat.

Norah and Eddie, two of the interns, are whispering

over by the wall where Dr. Diaz posts the schedules and charts for us. Buttoning up, I walk over to them.

"Are you sure they are going to announce?" Eddie asks in a low voice.

Norah shrugs, glancing at me.

"What did you hear?" I ask as though we haven't heard the rumors snaking through the halls for weeks now.

"It never adds up to anything," Norah scoffs. "I wouldn't hold my breath."

Eddie vigorously shakes his head in disagreement. "No, Mango has been whispering about this for a few weeks now."

I cock my head. Dr. Diaz is one of the lead scientists in the research group that named themselves Mango. Some story about one of the doctors bringing in dried mango and no one liking it except that it's the only snack left to eat at the end of the night so they all ate the mango. If there are hints from that group . . .

Norah jerks her chin at Eddie and gives him the dirty-eyeball stare. He presses his lips together and the two move away, whispering furiously at each other. I know Norah doesn't think I'm worthy of knowing the inside scoop. She likes playing quarterback in our little intern group, setting up after-work parties and getting all the gossip on the lead scientists. I haven't kissed her ass enough for her to warrant me an exclusive.

I try not to care about Norah's little jab and instead focus on searching for my assignment. Maybe it'll be a glamorous action-packed day of labeling blood work or wheeling carts of dirty test tubes, beakers, and equipment down to the sterilizing room. Anything is better than what I normally do, which is sit at a computer screen and input dates and numbers that don't make sense because it's part of some larger result that no one bothers to explain. Today Dr. Diaz has benevolently assigned me centrifuge duty. Boring as doing laundry, but at least it'll leave me time to catch up on some homework.

At first, it all seems very exciting being picked out of hundreds of applicants all over the city for this prestigious internship. It's couched with a certificate and a handshake while the local papers take pictures, but basically you are free labor. Another set of hands to do the grunt work. Because there is a lot of it. Even the scientists with certifiable PhDs and brains the size of boulders have to bow down and respect the hierarchy. There is always someone right above you who has the ability to command you at will. I've seen grown men with degrees from Yale and Harvard spitting mad enough to cry because they didn't get the approval or funding or whatever else they thought they deserved instead of the lowly task of replicating results to test for consistency.

I read over the chart to see what the other interns are doing. Norah, of course, has the best job today. She gets to record while they split some cells. That's the most exciting task out of all the chores. I suppose knowing what the leads like and baking them their favorite cookies gets you somewhere. I do have to hand it to Norah, though, she has drive about this work for some reason, not like most of the interns, who don't really care what the Genentium scientists do down here. For them, working in the lab is all about the quid pro quo. This will look great on their college applications, and hopefully, if they've cleaned their lead's goggles enough times, they might even get a paragraph-long letter out of it. The outcome is reassuring. The results predictable. Which is why I love this place. Everything has an order. Even the social network. There is nothing more soothing than knowing exactly where you stand, why, and how you can or cannot change it. Make a discovery and you are a rock star. Aid in an assist to a clue, or key insight, and you can swear off shit work for years. Sit on a winning team and you eat well. Feast or famine.

I walk into the large refrigerated room where vials of blood sit waiting to be centrifuged so the high-speed spinning will force the blood to separate into layers of plasma, white blood cells and platelets, and red blood cells. I check my list against the ones that I load onto my tray, each tube fitting neatly, perfectly, into its slot and grouping.

The centrifuge machines are located at the end of the hall. They sit outside randomly in front of various offices like they are copy machines. I load one group of tubes into one machine and set the timer for one hour. Down the hall at the second machine, I load the second group of vials and this time set the timer for thirty minutes. Back at the first machine I sit down on the floor to do my calculus homework. The low-decibel humming almost rocks me to sleep as I plow methodically through a dozen equations.

A set of footsteps echoes through the hall. I glance up and find myself staring at the guy with the animals from the elevator earlier. One hand is shoved into the pocket of his lab coat; the other one holds two vials.

"How long you going to be?" he asks.

I check my watch. "Another four minutes."

He nods and looks back down the hall as though trying to decide whether to wait or come back. He pushes back his shoulder-length, sun-bleached hair and checks his wristwatch. His white lab coat splays open, revealing a black T-shirt with a half-illuminated skull that looks like a waning moon if you glance at it quickly. Something caught in the air vent duct clicks the passing of time.

I return to my math. He moves closer to the centrifuge, eyeing the timer. He's clicking his tongue on the roof of his mouth. I can almost hear the saliva moving around. I put down my pencil.

"There's a free machine down the hall, past the C block offices."

He smiles and nods at me, but doesn't budge.

I go back to my math. He continues to click his tongue. There is such a slurping quality to the noise, I swear if I look up right at this moment I will find him making saliva bubbles with his mouth. I sneak a peek. He has turned his back to me.

"Do you mind?" I say.

He turns around. "What?"

I try to find his badge, which would tell me his name, but of course, he is too cool for requirements. "Could you stop making that noise?"

"What noise?'

"That clicking." I wave at my mouth and refrain from using an adjective to elaborate my disgust.

He presses his lips together and brings his finger up to his shocked face in a shushing motion. Jerk. I turn back to my math. And on closer inspection, I realize that his tan is not fake but real. The huge amount of peeling on the bridge of his nose, which I didn't see earlier in the dim lights of the elevator, attest to that. He must be a new lab tech from the state university. A group of them just started working on some work-study program.

He clears his throat.

I don't look up.

He starts talking anyway. "Is there a special feature on this machine?"

"What do you mean?" I ask, still scribbling away.

"Dr. Mendelson specifically underlined centrifuge number five on my instructions."

Now I look up. "Dr. Mendelson?"

He is checking out the machine, scanning the buttons. Dr. Mendelson doesn't let just any tech work with her. She is very specific about her team. In fact, you have to establish your brilliance before she even asks you to clean her equipment. Sunburn looks too young and definitely not brilliant enough to be taking orders from Dr. Mendelson. He finishes his inspection and steps back.

"What's so special about number five?" he asks.

I tuck a strand of hair behind my ear and think about whether or not I will answer him. Not everyone deserves to know everything. I continue to go over my homework, sitting in silence as though we are playing chicken to see who speaks first. He holds something out to me. I slide my eyes over. Bazooka.

Goddamn it, I love these hard-as-hell pieces of gum that make my jaw hurt so bad after five minutes of chewing that I start to believe I have TMJ. But they come with a comic, and how can anyone resist that? I take the gum.

He leans back against the wall and crosses his arms. I carefully unwrap the gum and pop it into my mouth as I look over the comic of the blond boy with an eye patch.

Not everyone knows how Dr. Mendelson has certain attachments, superstitions as it were, about the machines. This one, number five, Dad had it shipped over from the Salk Institute when he recruited her. Part of the sweetening package.

Sunburn makes that awful noise again with his mouth. I slip the comic into my lab coat pocket to read over later when I don't have to deal with a certain impatient slurping person.

"It was involved in helping her locate the repetition in the gene for Huntington's," I finally tell him.

He raises an eyebrow. "She definitely has her quirks,"

he says, "but with a mind like that, how can you not?"

I return to my math, chewing my hard-earned reward with some effort when I feel his eyes on me again. This time I refuse to make eye contact.

"Hey." Sunburn snaps his fingers. "We've met before, right?"

I ignore him.

"Where did we meet?" He directs the question more to himself than to me.

I can feel him leaning down as though he is getting ready to sit on the floor beside me. I check my watch again. Two more minutes.

Sunburn lowers himself down next to me and sits cross-legged, his hands in his lap, palms up. I see a large scar slashing across one palm and continuing over to the other as though someone pulled a sword blade through his hands. He catches me staring and balls them up into loose fists.

"It's so quiet out in the halls. It's kind of funny that they leave the machines out here," he says.

I have often thought the same thing.

"But I like it," he adds. "It's the only time I get to think. When I hear the hum of the machines and wait those last few minutes for the cycle to finish. You know?"

How many times have I found myself just standing here, staring at the swirling drum, caught in the cage of my thoughts?

"The cycle times," I say awkwardly. "Sometimes it's too

short to leave and come back, so you just end up hanging out."

"It's kind of a limbo place as you wonder what the results will be," he says. "Anything could happen."

I shrug. "Or nothing at all."

Our eyes meet as I finally look up from my notebook. The blueness startles me.

"I know I've seen your face somewhere. Damn. I hate that feeling of knowing it's on the edge of your brain. Did you have shorter hair before?"

The timer on the centrifuge machine beeps three times in quick succession. I close my notebook and grab my tray as I stand up.

"Do you ever hitchhike? I give lifts to people sometimes."

I shake my head, open the lid, and begin removing the vials and loading them onto my tray.

Sunburn scrambles up and gazes down at my badge.

"Grace." He snaps his fingers. "I saw your picture . . . at your house! I knew I recognized you."

I slowly place the last vial into its slot on my tray.

"Your father—he was the one who recruited me. He made me an offer I couldn't refuse. You know what I mean? He came all the way to Australia where I was on vacation, just so he could talk me into coming for a visit and interviewing. Can you believe that?"

Dad recruited Sunburn? So he wasn't from the university. A junior postdoc? Sunburn isn't the first to talk about how great Dad is. How much money and other perks he would throw into the deal to sweeten the offer. Dad's a master at that game. If he knows someone likes tennis, he'll always manage to get them a membership at the place with the best courts. Or if they like wines, he'll add onto their contract a weekend getaway to Sonoma during harvest season. Special equipment shipped across country for superstitions. Stuff like that makes all the difference. Not to mention the names he would throw around. The best people in their field. The best minds. Who wouldn't want to be associated with that?

"I'm Will, by the way." He holds out his hand. "I didn't know you worked here too."

I reach forward and shake his hand. The raised ridge of his scar feels hardened and tough. "I have an internship," I state, and then immediately wish I could take back my words.

"Ohhh, one of the coveted internships," he says with a smile, making me wonder whether he is teasing or insinuating that Dad helped me get this position.

Annoyance bundles my nerves, but I try not to show him any reaction as I lower the lid to the centrifuge. I don't have to justify myself to him or anyone around here.

"Grace." He shifts his balance back and forth. "Your dad, he saved my life during a really hard time. My sister had just died, and I didn't know what I was going to do. But he understood things about me. What I was feeling . . . I just want to say how much your dad—"

I turn on my heels. How dare he call it the coveted internship. *I'm* the one who got this internship. I didn't even use my full name, just so the judging would be fair. So they wouldn't recognize me as his daughter. I want to tell Will all this. Tell him that I earned this internship without any help. Instead I try to act nonchalant. Unfazed. Cool as the breeze blowing outside.

"All yours," I toss over my shoulder. I'm here because I belong here. Not because my father, who is not a researcher and insists on holding on to the most unrealistic hopes, got me a job. I begin counting the sound of my footfalls on the hard concrete floor to keep my mind off what Will is saying to me. Fifty-three steps that take me farther and farther away from all his insinuations. At the door to my lab, I stop and reach up to tie my hair back in a ponytail. I am a scientist and I know what is and is not within the realm of possibility. Hope is just a four-letter word.

WinterSpringSummer Autum

Fifty-one, fifty-two, fifty-three ... Her misaligned pig-tails shook every time she bowed her head rhythmically to the silent counting in her head as she peeled each paper muffin liner away from the stack. She pushed her tongue through the gap where her baby tooth had just fallen out. The rawness of her gum felt strange, but she couldn't help but worry that new empty spot. Daddy had promised a new tooth would soon grow in. She wondered how her body knew to shed things like a tooth and grow a new one in its place. Someday she would study the body and its cells just like her father and know everything about how it worked. She set down the muffin cup, making sure it was perfectly in line with the others. The ghostly ridged paper forms were in neat rows one after the other across the middle of the kitchen floor.

The high-pitched whistle of the noon freight train passing through town broke her concentration. She lifted her head, stopped her counting. Dropping the paper muffin cups, she raced over to the kitchen door. She threw open the door and a breeze whipped her pigtails back. Over the side fence, beyond the deserted parking lot, between the abandoned buildings, she spied the train cars slowly passing through the town as they traveled toward the port city 108 miles away. She began counting.

Her mother stood at the sink washing dishes, but once the cold air rushed inside, she turned and said, "Bugaboo, please close the door. It's close to thirty degrees outside."

She pretended not to have understood and kept the door open, continuing her counting until the final car passed out of sight. Twenty-three. A long train today. She would report that to her father when he came home, and they would mark it on her calendar beside her bed.

Her mother came to stand behind her and placed her warm, damp hands on the soft baby fat of her cheeks. "How many today?"

"Twenty-three."

Mama's eyes gazed out to the tracks. "That's too many."

She stared up at Mama's face. They used to count together, but more and more Mama didn't want to watch them the way they had when they first moved into the house. Mama had insisted on this house because she liked making sure she could see the trains. She said she needed to know they were real.

"Okay, bug. Let's close this door. It's freezing."

Mama shut the door to the brisk wind signaling the approaching winter and walked back to the sink. Along the way, she swiftly bent down, scooping up the muffin papers on the floor. "Bug, the muffins are already in the oven."

"But Mama, I was counting those."

Mama sighed and then slowly held them out.

She ran over and grabbed them.

Mama pointed to the small table in the corner covered with a cream tablecloth dotted with periwinkle-blue forget-me-nots. "It's too cold on the floor. Why don't you sit at the table?"

She nodded obediently and sat down. Her mother hated any kind of floor that did not have some form of carpet on it. Even at the sink, Mama wore slippers as she stood on a fuzzy floor mat. Mama hated her feet being cold. Said it reminded her of a place that she had lived in once upon a time. Once upon a time, so long ago.

She licked her thumb and rubbed the crinkly paper between it and her pointer finger, trying to separate each liner from the next. Mama sang softly as she finished washing the rest of the dishes. The running water muffled the words, but she could still hear the melody. She hummed along to Mama's song as she counted. Without the door open to the breeze, the bright sun streaming through the windows warmed the tiny kitchen, thickening the scent of the buttery muffins baking in the oven. She glanced at the timer sitting on the counter. One more minute and the muffins would be ready. She scowled at the remaining muffin papers in her hand. She had better hurry. Her heart raced as she counted, her ears straining to hear every click of the timer. Fifty-four, fifty-five, fifty-six. The train whistle echoed faintly one last time in the background.

Winter Spring SummerAutum

The distant howl of the train splits the night. Long, piercing shrieks slicing through my mind. I look up from the homework that I am trying to finish before bed and leap from my desk. Run to the window. But as I part the curtain, my fingers trembling, my eyes close shut.

Strange, how the body knows instinctually to protect itself. Eyes blinking before the blast of sand. Arm rising before the blow. The will to survive is not a conscious choice, but encoded into every cell. The body acts to defend and protect itself even against one's own mind.

I force my eyes open to confront the darkness. The cold reassures me as I lean my forehead against the pane of glass and stare out into the frozen landscape barely illuminated by the crescent moon. We live so far from anything. Just meadows and trees as far as the eye can see. Out here, even the sound of a passing car is an event. Legions of bare fields surround me. I am an island.

The scream of the train recedes until the high-pitched whistle only echoes like an abandoned TV talking to itself in the other room. Perspiration pools under my arms, a drop rolling down the side of my rib cage until it soaks into the cotton of my T-shirt. I let the curtain fall back into place.

There are no train tracks. I know this for a fact. A conscious fact that I repeat to myself over and over again as I sit on my bed and open the nightstand drawer. Inside, there is a black journal and pen. I need to keep track of what is happening. I check my clock and note the time: 1:07 a.m.

As I leaf through the pages, searching for the last entry, my heart fists when I see all the notes. The pages are filled with my handwriting, each entry dated and notated. Some days there are multiple entries about moving shadows in my peripheral vision, clanking noises from radiators that are not in this house, but from two houses ago. On other pages, there's just one entry, mostly about missing Dad as he traveled, but those were at the beginning of the journal. The recent entries are short, sometimes just one word, "train," with a date next to it. By the end, all my handwriting crowds together, one entry flowing into the other like codes of data. Though I know I am the only one logging this information, I cannot remember how the pages have gotten filled. How can I have no memory of entering these notes? And now there is no more room in the journal. I stare at my handwriting and a realization forces my lips together against the nausea. There are only a few possibilities for this disorientation, this lapse of memory. And I know them as well as I know this house. I have researched extensively. The first time when I was old enough to understand why and how my mother could have abandoned me. The next time when I started this journal. But to lose track of all the entries, the compromised state of my memory . . . This is another piece of evidence that I cannot ignore.

Sitting on the edge of the mattress, my feet placed firmly on the ground, I force myself to feel the frigid wooden floors. Force my thoughts, my ears to the other noises in the house. The creaks and movements, each physical sound a reminder of where I am. This room, this house, this place. My reality comes into focus.

I don't scare easily, having lived in so many cities and countrysides of one kind or another. But a house so completely removed from any noise of civilization seemed, at first, uncanny. Only over the last few months have I grown used to this place. I know the blueprint of each room, having charted every sound meticulously, like a doctor hunting for a disease. The popping in the attic comes from a crossbeam that only moves when the wind is strong enough to dip the birch saplings in the field. A ticking from downstairs like a cartoon time bomb signals that the woodstove is cooling down and the baseboard heaters are warming up. The spastic seasonal rattle in the window above the kitchen sink has only been quiet on the most humid summer days, when the wood swollen with moisture shuts down on itself. Every little noise registers as though the house is talking to me.

I slip my cold feet under the sheets and pull the comforter over my shoulders before lying back. Though spring has officially started, winter grips on by its fingernails. My frozen hands slide neatly under my pillow, the cool envelope making me sigh. I force my eyes shut, but my mind continues to roam.

If I concentrate, really focus my mind, I can even hear, down the hall, the rhythmic, guttural exhale of my father sleeping. Not exactly a snore, but not just loud breathing. It's the sound of a reluctant sneaker scraping across the blacktop at the end of recess. Even in his sleep, my father regrets the lost hours when he could be working, researching, coming, going, doing something. Anything. To keep from feeling. This place.

The middle place. Not death. Not life. A limbo state of existence filled with the hours of turning the wheels. Eating to not feel hungry. Sleeping to not feel tired. Waking to not feel asleep. The middle place that exists between breaths, in that pause, that slight breathlessness before an exhale and an inhale. Between the crest and the valley. Where the path always meanders cliffside.

How much longer will I be able to endure? How much longer will I have a choice? Or is it all a mirage? Our mind tricking us, showing us what we need to see in order to live just a moment longer? Is that truly our free will, our conscious choice? And what of love? Does love allow us to choose? In my leaving, the one who will suffer the most is not me, but him. Aren't all our decisions swaddled and nestled next to those we love?

I remind myself of where I am. Lying here in my bed. Right here. Clutching my pillow and breathing in the scent of the laundry detergent, my own salty sweat, and the faint musty odor of this old house. My house. I force my thoughts to charting the rhythmic mechanical clanking of my house. Slowly my breathing steadies, and the haunting nightmare of the train relinquishes its hold. I feel myself on the edge of consciousness and unconsciousness, and the longing for sleep to steal me away, even if only for a few hours, chokes my throat.

This is not living. This is existing. I feel myself standing at the precipice, looking back at the shadow I cast, looking forward into an emptiness that holds no light. I know I cannot stay here much longer. In this place. This place where the train still shrieks.

Vinter SpringSummerAutumn

Had I been wrong to hope, then?

The first time I saw you swaying, your fist clenched against your lips, your neck straining, moving to the metronome of your mind like waves crashing over and over against rocks, I reached out to steady you before calling your name. I watched your eyes enlarge, your head swiveling violently all around as though searching for a lost thing.

I knew. I knew. I knew then in my heart when you could not answer me, what I refused to see for so long. But I couldn't let myself believe it. There had to be other explanations. I started insisting you go to sleep earlier. I kept the television on all the time so you would know the noises were real. I reminded you to shower. To eat. I pretended not to see the fatigue in your eyes as you pushed back against yourself.

What was I to do? What would you have had me do? After everything we had endured. Suffered. Loved. What was I to do? Tell myself the truth? That I was slowly losing you? That each day would close another room in your mind until all that was left was the skin of you? How could I live this way? Unable to reach you. Unable to let you go. Unable to do anything but wait. Wait. For you to return to me. A glimpse was all that I prayed for. Those moments would be enough. I would make them enough. We would beat down the wings of the Fates again. And again. And again.

Winter Spring Summer Autumn

The keyboard protests loudly as I pound out a quick reply to the e-mail from Dr. Diaz. Another late meeting along with a million attachments that I am supposed to read before signing a nondisclosure agreement later tonight after the announcements. I glance at the time and stand up quickly. I'll be late picking up Hannah if I don't hurry.

At the top of the stairs, a light-headed fluttering almost buckles my knees, making me grab the banister to steady myself. Not enough sleep makes me dizzy with fatigue. I pause to take a breath and then step carefully down the stairs. When I enter the kitchen, I find Dad already standing at the counter.

I notice the bagginess of his suit. He has gotten very thin recently. Which reminds me to ask about dinner. He never seems to eat enough, always leaving behind plates of untouched food as he stares into his laptop.

"Hey, Dad," I say.

"Hmm," he says, his eyes scanning the screen.

"DAD."

He looks up at me, a frown interrupting the smooth plane of his forehead. "Why are you yelling at me so early in the morning?"

I look away. I hate when he acts as though I'm the one being unreasonable. I turn back to him once my irritation is in check. "Dad, I have a late meeting at the lab tonight. Can you pick up dinner?"

He is focused again on the computer screen, his index and middle finger scrolling down the touchpad.

I walk over to him and pass my hand over his eyes. He glances up at me.

"Dad, I need you to be present for one minute," I say.

An awkward, embarrassed smile lifts the right corner of his upper lip. He brushes his hand over his face as though to rearrange his features and steps back from the computer screen to lean up against the counter.

"What's up, bugaboo?" His eyes are full beams.

I smile despite my annoyance. For all his distractions and busy schedule, when Dad wants to know something, really concentrates on something or someone, even the sun seems weak.

"I have a late meeting tonight. Pick up something for dinner, okay?"

He tilts his head. "Late meeting? At the lab? Isn't that kind of unusual?"

Now it's my turn to act distracted. I walk over to the coffee machine and start making the coffee.

Dad walks over and crouches down, trying to study my face. I know he is looking to read me like he does with everyone he meets. It's his job to know what other people are thinking before they even have a chance to say it to themselves.

"Dr. Mendelson thinks she has something, doesn't she?"

To keep from meeting his stare, I focus on the slow drip of coffee and run over the ratio of ground beans to water for the optimal caffeine extraction.

"You don't have to say anything."

It has been a while since the lab has been on high alert; the gossip mill churning while everyone looks for signs. It is still too early. Nothing definitive. If anything, it is even more questionable, since in the end, everything, all the tests, all the results, the data, will have to be documented and replicated and tested again and again. We are only beginning, yet even that fact holds power. Hope unchained is a beast.

The drip slows to a halt and I reach up into the cupboard to pull down two mugs. As soon as I set them on the counter and reach for the coffeepot, he pounces and catches my eyes.

Dad pumps one fist into the air. "Goddamn it. She is brilliant. I knew she was going to change that lab around. But in one year. Who would have even guessed? Goddamn it."

"Dad, you can't say anything. Absolutely nothing. Interns only get the gossip, not the real briefings. Nothing is for sure, okay? This meeting could just be about announcing some new clinical trial or something."

"Gracie, come on. Give me some credit here. How long have I been in this business? Ten, twelve years? Besides, that's why they have corporate in an entirely different building. So we don't pressure you geek types." Dad turns to his computer screen and his fingers fly over his keyboard.

"How about pizza tonight?" I ask.

Dad mutters, "This could be the link. This could be the opening for the next round of clinical trials. I can't believe she did it in a year."

Watching him work in such excitement reminds me of all the other times when he thought he was onto something. Back then, when I was younger, I could lean against him and he would reach out with one hand to pull me close while with his other hand he typed out a final sentence. Then he would hug me. Lift me up onto the counter and sit me in front of him to talk. Really talk. About the too many movies and TV shows I was watching and how come I had no friends. Sometimes after those conversations, he would rush around and sign me up for

tennis or pottery or ukulele lessons. Only he would forget
what day, what time, and I would end up either missing
them, or worse, sitting there waiting, feeling abandoned
because he forgot to pick me up again as the sympathetic
or annoyed eyes of strangers gazed down at me. After a
while, I stopped complaining and learned that reading at
home was just as good as any friend.

Now I move away from his frenetic energy. This need
that consumes every day of his life. All for love. For us.
For me. The exhaustion creeps across my shoulders, drips
down my spine.

Before heading out to the car, I yell back, "Don't forget
the pizza."

Silence.

I resist the urge to yell again and simply pick up my
backpack by the door and head out. If nothing else, we can
have soup. There is always soup in the house. I have come
to hate soup.

When I drive by the place I usually pick up Hannah, at
the cross stop where the dirt road meets the paved one,
and find it empty, I know she is still angry. She has never
let me drive her home, so I don't know where she lives.
And I can't call her because she doesn't own a cell phone.
Every time I tried to push my old one on her, she would
get angry until she finally shouted that her family couldn't
afford those things. I stare down the dirt road and wish so
badly to see her walking toward me. I want to cry the way

Toad probably did when Frog left him. If Hannah would forgive me, I would eat all the soggy sandwiches in the world. At school I search the halls, but there is no sign of her. Dave Riley can't be found either. In AP Chemistry, I overhear a girl named Gloria talking to her lab partner, Beth.

"Why didn't I sign up to go on the Costa Rica trip?" Gloria complains.

"Because we have an AP exam in a month. And you know it's a god squad trip." Beth carefully titrates some hydrochloric acid into the sodium hydroxide base. "That was another milliliter."

Gloria jots it down in her notebook. "I don't know why we're considered the smart ones when we're stuck here while they're in ninety-degree tropical heat and swimming with sea turtles."

"Oh, stop whining. They're doing missionary work. They aren't on the beach lying around. They're supposed to be building some damn church in the mountains. That's why the trip is free."

"You have a point," Gloria says, and turns back to her notebook.

I calculate the millimeters for the acid-to-base ratio for the titration and wonder if Hannah has gone on that trip with Dave. He would have gone, since he is a part of that Methodist church group. Maybe Hannah signed up at the last minute to go with him? If only people were as predictable as chemical reactions.

My only comfort of the day comes when I drive into Genentium's parking lot. Here I have a role. A function that is bigger than just breathing for living's sake. Here there is a purpose for me. I enter the building ready to control my mind and focus on results. It's going to be a big day for Genentium. For Dad. But what if Norah is right and all of it will just come to nothing?

At the end of the day shift, everyone whispers and rushes down the hall toward the announcements. The meeting doesn't take place in the conference room, but instead, everyone crowds into Dr. Mendelson's lab. The senior scientists gather at one end of the room, and the rest of us push in where there is space between the workstations and the rows of desks. I can barely see into the room. I lean left, then right, hoping for a glimpse of the doctors at the front.

Someone wonders, "Why aren't we meeting in the conference room?"

"Top secret stuff," someone in the back says. "That room could be bugged."

"Shhh!" Dr. Diaz shoots her laser beams around the room, trying to identify the culprits.

I hoist myself onto a lab counter and sit so I can see over the taller people's heads. Dr. Mendelson is flanked by two other senior researchers. She raises both of her hands and begins to wave. Her shining halo of blond hair and wide brown eyes make her look almost elfin. Except when she's concentrating, which is almost always, and then her eyes take on a demonic quality that makes one step back when she approaches.

"Settle down, everyone," she booms.

It's disconcerting to hear such a trucker's voice coming from a short, middle-aged woman.

The entire room stills and readies itself for the news that has been creeping through the labs.

"Now, some of you may have been privy to the latest round of gossip. I want to address these rumors." Dr. Mendelson takes her time, eyes locking on various faces around the room.

Will is leaning against a counter on the far left side of the room. He catches me glancing at him and winks. I quickly revert my attention back to Dr. Mendelson.

"There has been a development." She lowers her voice. "The information that I am about to share with you cannot leave this building. All of you will be asked to sign a document before leaving tonight."

A few people shuffle their feet. Someone in the back claps briefly. Another complains, "We already signed a confidentiality agreement when we came to work here."

Dr. Mendelson barks out a laugh like a seal and seems to know exactly where to look when she says, "Well, now you'll be doubly careful about opening your big mouth."

She smiles serenely and waits a few beats, allowing the room to grow tense in anticipation. Finally, after another pass with her eyes, she continues.

"Tomorrow we will be announcing that C4-511 will

commence a phase one clinical drug trial."

Shoulders begin to slump with the announcement; the phase one trial was expected, even late. After all, the approvals from the FDA had been posted last summer. The latest antipsychotic drug was just a minor victory, but a useful one for funding, Dad had said. With the anticlimactic announcement, restlessness descends. I lean forward, watching all the scientists whispering to one another like schoolkids at a boring assembly.

Dr. Mendelson is pacing back and forth as though she is thinking. Suddenly she stops. "Nothing is certain." She runs her hands through her hair and then places them palms together, as though in prayer. "We are at a momentous point in this lab."

A ripple of silence spreads across the room. A few people lean forward.

Dr. Mendelson lowers her hands. "We are on the cusp of history. Each procedure, each measurement, each move that you make will either aid or detract from this occasion. Each one of you can and will make a difference." She pauses, letting her words expand and grow. "We believe we have located a gene. SIC-5 holds the key to understanding how the other cluster of risk genes play a role in the development of schizophrenia."

My heart stops beating as I gasp. A gene. I can hear the distant slam of a door closing. The slight scrape of a chair leg on the concrete floor. The brush of denim rubbing together as a leg is crossed.

A lightning charge passes through the room. A few stand up from their chairs, craning to see Dr. Mendelson's face. "This is the critical juncture. We need everyone on board. This is the Rosetta Stone."

I can feel the energy swirling around me. The air becomes thick with voices. They found a universal genetic marker. How many years has Dad been waiting for this news? How many jobs? How many moves? How many years of hoping? Does this news change anything? A wave of nausea makes my mouth fill with saliva. The past is the past and nothing can bring her back.

Dr. Mendelson raises one hand and beckons. "I need senior scientists in my office in ten minutes. The rest of you can sign the paperwork that will be waiting for you out in the hall. Thank you, everyone."

Voices erupt.

"Did she just say what I thought she said?"

"Which test group? Mango?"

"I heard it was Richardson's group, Odin."

"I heard it was Dillon's."

"That prick."

I let the crowd of hips and shoulders carry me toward the door. The cavernous hallway begins to fill with people. Everyone is talking about the SIC-5 gene. How many of us have been working on that discovery without even knowing?

At first all I can do is stand there. Even as I feel people brush past me, I stand in place, waiting for the world to stop spinning. Along one side of the hallway, a few of the office people from upstairs are standing behind folding tables loaded with papers. The excited chatter of the discovery reaches a crescendo.

I walk to the far end of the hall. Safely away from everyone, I lean my back against the wall and let my legs finally buckle beneath me. As I sink to the ground, I taste the first warm, salty tears. They found it. I clutch my legs and press my forehead to my knees.

Mama, they found it.

"Mama," she called.

Her mother stood at the sink, her face turned toward the window. She had been standing there for such a very long time. Standing without moving or even breathing, it seemed. She was so still the light moved over her like an empty chair in the living room.

"Mama," she called again. The timer had been ringing nonstop and still Mama did not move.

The glass window into the oven revealed nothing except the doomed crowned circles that she imagined blackening and darkening into pieces of coal as she watched helplessly. It had happened before. Too many times. The only thing Mama never burned was soup, and that was because it was from a can.

She sniffed at the air. The muffins were burning. She knew it. She reached for her mother's elbow and pulled hard on her arm.

Her mother blinked as though waking from a dream, her eyes adjusted to the new scene in front of her, growing wide in her realization of the noise invading the kitchen. She raced to the oven and shut off the timer.

"They are fine. Just fine. Just fine. Fine. They are fine," Mama said over and over again as she slipped on the oven mitts and threw open the oven door. A blast of hot air blew out.

"Move away," her mother said, pulling the muffins out of the oven.

She wouldn't budge from her spot, waiting anxiously to inspect the muffins. Miraculously, they were not burnt. Brown and slightly darker on the edges. But not burnt.

Mama set the muffins on top of the stove. "You didn't have to pull on my arm so hard."

"The timer was ringing, Mama."

"I heard it. I did." Mama pointed at the muffins. "Look, they came out just fine."

"You were going to burn them again. Like all the other times," she accused.

Mama's smile melted drop by drop. First her forehead, then her eyes, her cheeks, and finally her lips. Mama's chin dropped into her chest and she blinked rapidly. She spoke in a soft voice. "But I didn't burn them."

Mama turned suddenly and shuffled in her slippers over to the back kitchen door with the oven mitts still on her hands. The way she just stood there, looking out the window of the closed door without moving to open it or even bothering to take off the oven mitts, filled the air with unease.

The strangeness of Mama made her feel guilty and mean. She walked over to Mama and grabbed her around the middle, laying her cheek on the small of Mama's back.

"I'm sorry, Mama," she said. "The muffins are not burnt."

Mama's cartoon hands slowly lifted up and patted her arms.

"It's starting to snow," Mama whispered.

Outside, the first snow of the season gently drifted down, then swirled back up, caught in a breeze. Her mother swayed back and forth as though she was trapped by the same wind. A low guttural moan escaped Mama's lips. "The train is coming."

Vinter **Spring** SummerAutumn

The sun, low on the horizon, illuminates the last lingering drifts of spring snow as the harsh wind swirls it high into the air until the tiny flecks of white are lost to the oblivion above. The streets are empty save for a few hurried people who walk with their heads down, their coats cinched tight. I pull my hat over my ears and start toward the parking lot behind Genentium. It's not late, but most everyone has cleared out to celebrate after signing the paperwork. I shove my hands deep into my pockets. For years they had believed they were getting closer. First they had identified clusters, but there had to be a gene. I stare ahead of me, the street stretching off into the distance. Dad has been waiting for this news for over a decade, and the last thing I want to do is talk to him. I veer left, walking away from the lab.

A lone figure stands under the concrete eaves of a building, off to the side behind the bus stop bench. Hood pulled down low, head swaying to the beat of the music emanating from the phone held in one hand. With each movement, I can see the music like waves of heat floating above asphalt summer streets. Bass smooth and deep, peppered with guitar riffs that speak to the feet. Each beat. Each crest. Each slide. The notes are flames, flickering warmth against the windswept streets. As I approach, the music becomes clearer and I begin to hear a voice, low and strong.

> *"Did you die last night only to be reborn with*
> *dawn's light?*
> *Into this skin you wear.*
> *Eyes that can't see. Ears that can't hear. A mind*
> *that holds no truth.*
> *You died but forgot to leave.*
> *The past crawls into the present, birthing the*
> *future.*
> *Shell-shocked. Shell locked. And all the*
> *answers.*
> *On the inside.*
> *Your mind mirrors.*
> *A kaleidoscope.*
> *You inside you inside you."*

I step quickly, but in that second before I pass, before my next footfall carries me away, rendering this moment a blade of grass in the landscape of my memory, the hood falls back. All the seasons of her life in those eyes.

"Mama?" I step forward in shock.

The woman glances down and the resemblance disappears instantly.

"Sorry," I mutter, and stumble back. "I thought you were someone else."

I walk away quickly, trying to shake off what just happened. It was the announcement, I tell myself. The announcement and what it would have meant to her if she had been around. But even as I try to convince myself, the words that the woman spoke have already stolen inside and my body shivers in recognition. Fate is but an encrypted code of genes. Your chromosomes a map of the future that cannot be changed. Only fought. Battles lost. Battles won. Reprieve. Parlay. A deep ache of loneliness overwhelms me, and I am almost brought to my knees in one breath. I turn around and walk back to the woman on the street, but when I return to the bus bench, the street is empty.

My vision blurs as I search for the exact place where she was standing, press my fingertips to my eyes and then lower my hands. There is no trace of her. Even her footprints have been erased by the windswept snow. I shiver and head back toward the Genentium parking lot. Within a block I know that I have missed it. How did I miss it?

I peer at the street signs as though they are written in another language. How could I be on the wrong street? I've walked to this parking lot dozens of times now. I pull off my wool hat and let the cold night air seep into my skull. The freezing wind does nothing to shake my dizziness. Stop it. I know where I'm going. I examine the streets and buildings. This way. I step off the curb to head in the direction I believe is right, but I am seized by a fear. A sensation of falling. I am lost.

After walking and walking, trying to remember where I am, my body begins to protest. My hands have turned a bone white and my fingers refuse to move. I step inside a diner to ask for directions. The warmth hits me, solid as knuckles on cheekbone. How long have I been walking? I carefully ease onto a stool at the counter. A waitress walks over, her eyes lighting on my face.

"Hey, sweetie, you're here pretty late. Want a cup of coffee?"

"Sure," I say. I look around, unnerved by a sense of familiarity. It feels like I should know this, but I can't remember. The waitress walks over with a coffeepot in her hand. She slides over a mug and proceeds to pour.

"It's been a while, Grace. The lab keeping you busy?"

I stare at her name card, Stephanie. Stephanie. Why can't I remember her? She knows me. Knows my name. Where I work. My heart races in panic. I live in Jericho, Illinois. My father is Joseph King. I am Grace King.

"Stephanie, where is Genentium?"

Stephanie stares at me for a moment and then smiles. "Funny, Grace."

She turns around and heads back to the kitchen, pushing open the swinging door and stepping past as it sways like a pendulum, moving back and forth, back and forth. And with each pass, I see less and less of Stephanie.

She walks around the kitchen filled with pots and pans hanging from the ceiling. Talks to the cook holding a frying pan. Picks up a few plates. Pivots around. Sees. Me.

The door returns to its resting position and the world beyond my world is closed. And in that moment of yearning for just another glimpse, I remember what I had forgotten. I remember. Being here with Dad. Stephanie laughing and pouring us coffee before going back to the kitchen and bringing out our food. The way Dad always remembered to bring her M&M's from the corner store when he got his cigarettes. The realization doubles and folds, origamis inside me until I have to lean my cheek against the cool counter, refusing to see what I already know.

Genentium is across the street.

WinterSpringSummer Autum

The swinging door between the kitchen and the dining room swayed back and forth. She pushed it again, trying not to bother Mama about when the muffins would be cool enough to eat. They were still in the tin, sitting on top of the stove. She stared at Mama just sitting there at the oval table, the oven mitts still on her hands. Mama kept glancing around the room, every now and then quietly whispering as though she were speaking with someone. How much longer would Mama be there? she wondered. But if she asked again, she knew Mama would get angry. Maybe even yell at her. She pushed open the door again, before letting it go and watching Mama's face appear and disappear with each pass.

The sound of a car pulling into the driveway took her away from studying Mama. The back kitchen door opened.

"DADDY!" she yelled in surprise and delight.

He walked in and set down his bag before picking her up under the arms and swinging her high into the air. Weightless joy swept back her hair, and she grinned as she reached for his face. Only he was strong enough to carry her like a baby again. He kissed the top of her head and released her back to the earth as Mama walked into the kitchen.

"What are you doing home?" Mama asked as he walked over to her. Dad leaned forward and gathered her in his arms. For a moment, watching her parents like that, it seemed nothing in the world mattered to her mother and father except standing there, in each other's arms.

Mama pulled back and whispered, "It's hard today."

"Daddy"—she pulled on the sleeve of his shirt—"Mama made muffins."

Dad smiled down at her. "Enough for me, too?"

She nodded. "We made twelve. Twelve muffins are more than enough for three people."

"I don't know," Dad joked. "I'm pretty hungry."

Mama moved quickly then, setting out a plate, placing a muffin in the center, and bringing it over to the table. "Bug, come sit down and eat your muffin while your dad and I talk." Mama turned and walked back through the swinging door to the living room. Her father picked up his bag and followed her mother.

Her parents disappeared so fast it left her breathless for a moment. She stood in her place and for that space in time, it felt as though she'd never had parents. That she had always been alone in an empty room her entire life. Waiting to be found.

She knew it couldn't be true, but the feeling of it stayed with her as she walked slowly over to the table and sat down. All her earlier excitement and anguish about the muffin had cooled. Yet still, she had said she wanted the muffin and she was not a girl to go back on her words. Carefully she peeled back the wrapper, noticing the way the grooves in the paper were almost etched into the side. The buttery crumbs coated her fingers and she raised them to her lips to lick them off. They tasted strange, not as sugary as the ones from the bakery in town, but maybe homemade ones were not as sweet. She peeled the rest of the paper off and lifted the muffin to her lips for her first bite.

The gagging was immediate. A reflex of disgust. She spat. Coughed out the soggy pieces of muffin onto the table and glared as though they had just bitten her tongue. Maybe she had picked a bad spot. She wondered if muffins, like bananas or pears, could be pockmarked with bruises. She turned the muffin and timidly took another bite. The sharp, bitter sting of salt flooded her mouth again. She smashed the muffin onto her plate and then marched over to the swinging door, pushing it open with all her strength.

Her parents were on the couch in the living room, just beyond the dining room table. Her father's back blocking her view of her mother.

"Mama, I want some milk."

In his hand, the thin shaft of a needle gleamed and caught a glint of light.

"Bug," he said, "why don't you get me a muffin?" He spoke without turning back to look at her.

Her anger immobilized her. How could her parents just forget about her? How could her mother have baked such a monstrosity? The unfairness of it all crested over her until she felt that she would cry.

"NOW!" Mama yelled.

She jumped and ran through the still softly swinging door. She glanced back and saw her father take her mother's hand. Place Mama's palm against his cheek. The door finally stopped swinging. She was alone once more. An orphan of time.

Winter **Spring** SummerAutum

The light flickers before my eyes as a hand moves back and forth across my vision. I blink and meet his eyes. The blueness sinks into me, cutting off all my thoughts. Move. I need to get up from this diner counter, but the eyes are on me. He sits right next to me, but I have no memory of how he came to be beside me.

"Hey, Grace," he says.

I stare at him.

"It's Will." He makes a gross smacking sound with his mouth.

I smile.

"You were completely zoned out. I thought you were sleeping with your eyes open."

I stare down at my coffee mug. I don't want him to know how disoriented I feel. "Yeah, I'm pretty tired." I command myself to flash him another smile as I dig out a few dollars from my pocket. Smoothing out the wrinkled bills, I leave them on the counter and stand up.

"Are you leaving? Want to walk to the parking lot together?"

"I know where my car is."

Will squints at me. "Okay. Well, I'm headed home. Let's walk together."

There is a prickling of annoyance itching the back of my neck, but I try to let it go. He's trying to be nice, I remind myself. "Sure, whatever you want."

As we head to the door, Stephanie waves to us. I raise my hand just as Will raises his, and our elbows collide.

"Oww." Will laughs. "Are you sure you don't have a dagger hidden up your sleeve?"

A memory flashes through my mind. The way Dad would touch my mother's elbows, teasing her gently about the sharpness of her bones.

"Engineered for self-defense," I say, repeating my mother's line before I can stop the moment of déjà vu.

Will touches my elbow and then pushes open the door to the diner so that I can step outside.

The cold forces us to walk quickly, shoulder to shoulder. The blue-gray Genentium sign looms over us from across the street like a billboard. I try not to think about how I could have missed it. We quickly cross over.

There are only a few cars left in the parking lot when we arrive. Will points to one in the distance. "I'm over there," he says, glancing at me.

I see my black Lincoln in the corner.

"You good to drive home? I could give you a lift," he says as if I have been drinking or something.

"I'm fine. Why? Did Stephanie say something to you?" The prickling is now a full-blown heat rash. "Jesus, I got cold. It made me groggy. I don't know why she was making such a big deal. Why can't you people just leave me alone?" I say through gritted teeth.

Will holds up his hands in defense. "Hey, wait. Don't be paranoid. Steph just suggested that I walk you to your car because it was so late. We've all been celebrating."

"I haven't." I narrow my eyes and choose my words carefully. "Why would I want to celebrate something that is nothing but a fantasy?"

"Or the beginning of an arduous but incredible chance for treatment and hope." Will gestures with one hand like a game show host.

"You sound like my dad," I scoff.

Will grins. "I'm taking that as a compliment."

I turn around to head to my car. Will taps me on the shoulder. "You sure you're okay?" The intensity of his stare makes me feel like I am being examined.

The spark of annoyance blazes into anger. What does he want? I feel myself trembling. I want to explain how being disoriented doesn't make you crazy, but if I start talking, I know I am not going to make any sense. I shift back and forth on my feet and take a deep breath. Keep it together, I tell myself.

"Have a good night," I tell him, then move as though I am being chased and jump inside my car, slamming the door behind me. Calm down, I order myself. Calm down. Quickly I turn on the ignition and cup my hands over the heating vent. Slowly my fingers regain their feeling.

Every time I blink, I see the concern in Will's face. He knows something is wrong. I glance over my shoulder at the spot where we were standing. He is still there, watching me.

He holds up his hand as though placing it against a pane of glass. The invisible wall that separates him from me. From who I am and who he is. I place my palm against the freezing glass in response and he finally turns, jogging off toward his car. His slow, easy gait reminds me of summer days and the way I would run on the beach along the edge of the water.

The house is dark when I get home.

"Dad?"

I walk into the kitchen from the mudroom after hanging up my coat and call out again. "Dad."

The cold permeates my entire being. It's got to warm up soon, I think, and flick on the lights in the kitchen before filling the kettle with water for some tea. As I watch the electric coil of the burner slowly begin to glow from black to red, I think about Stephanie and Will. Their eyes wide with worry. I brush away the memory and remind myself, I was just taking a walk, burning off some steam. Except for my trembling hand as I take the kettle off the stove, I am convinced.

Dad's full cup of coffee sits cold on the counter next to his laptop. Every morning I pour him a cup and every morning he takes two sips before he forgets everything, staring into the screen. I pour the black liquid down the drain and search the counters for the pizza carton. I sigh. It's soup again. He is probably asleep in the living room.

I walk into the dark room and listen closely for his breathing. At first I hear nothing, but after a moment of concentration, I hear him breathing softly from the couch. And with that sound, all the cold disappears. I stand there, just listening, letting all the sounds of the house and Dad's breathing calm me.

I reach over and turn on the light. A pair of black-socked feet, crossed at the ankles and propped up on the armrest of the couch, peek out at me. The side lamp casts shadows, half illuminating the wall of photos above the woodstove. I glance up at the frozen memories.

The three of us on the beach in Los Angeles. Mama looking to the side as she lounges back in a chair, her hair windblown and messy. Dad holds me on his lap and cups the roundness of Mama's shoulder as she leans away from him. That was the last photo we took together before Mama disappeared. . . .

Dad had immediately shifted into military mode, working with the police and a private detective. Not to mention all his army buddies coming and going. The house was transformed into a mission base. I hid, mostly under the kitchen table, playing chess against myself.

Dad and I waited for years in that house by the train tracks. Waited for her to come home or the police to find her. All those Sundays in the car, driving across the city. I knew every single neighborhood in Los Angeles. Until the day he read that article on Huntington's, which was when he decided to leave and find her a different way. We moved so many times for all his leads on different labs and scientists, I stopped counting.

"Dad," I say, and walk over to the couch.

The feet uncross and I hear him clear his throat.

"What time is it, Grace?" Dad says, and sits up, his hands running through his hair.

"Late." I walk over to the woodstove next to the couch and start making a fire. We are low on wood. How can this be spring? "It's freezing in here."

"Hmmm," he says, as though he can't feel the cold. Or doesn't care. "The meeting ran that late?"

"Yeah," I answer faintly, and try to change the subject. I stop loading the stove and ask, "What happened to the pizza, Dad?"

He answers my question with a question. "What did Dr. Mendelson say?"

I scowl at him. "You forgot."

He nods, but his eyes are fastened on a formal black-and-white photo of my parents in some photographer's studio back in Korea. "What was the announcement?"

I refuse to answer. We both gaze up at the photo. My mother's skin is so flawless it looks porcelain. Her hair is swept up into a loose bun, her thick bangs curled just above her eyes. I can feel Dad watching me, his eyes moving from her face to mine.

"You look a lot like her," he says for the millionth time. Just like all the other times when I come and sit with him as he stares up at her pictures, recalling the memories that forever flood his mind.

"I miss her so much," my father says.

I study the gentle smile on her face.

"Did I ever tell you about the time—"

"She was the only one who could speak enough English to help you while you tried to save the Marine who got stabbed in the bar where she was working."

Dad smiles at me. "I guess I told you that one."

"No, actually, I think Mama did. She said you didn't look like an army doctor, even though you said you were. She thought you were trying to impress her after you followed her in your car as she was walking into town."

"I was off duty that day. And I wanted to make sure she stayed safe."

"Well, Mama said you were the worst-dressed American she had ever seen."

Dad looks hurt. "I didn't have a lot clothes in the foster

system. In Korea was the first time I had some money to myself. I thought I was looking sharp."

I smile. "Mama said that was why she fell in love with you. She knew you needed her."

Dad's sheepish grin makes him look exactly the way Mama described when they first met. He runs his hand over the top of his head like he is still feeling his buzz cut from his military days. "Your mom could make rags look like high fashion and then turn around and memorize whole chemistry textbooks for her nursing exams. When your mother wanted something, she was unstoppable. She was so strong. At least I had a few homes, but your mother in that orphanage . . . I don't know how she survived."

Their love story is one that I know front to back, back to front. I am the only blood relation either one of them has ever known.

"Sometimes I can feel every second lost. Every second that I could be working to make a difference. To bring her back," he says.

"Dad, don't do this to yourself."

"Grace, don't worry too much about me."

I shake my head. "How long are you going to be able to keep this up? How many more years can you work like this?"

"As long as it takes," he says.

The anger rising as bile at his fantasy world scorches my face. I stand and begin to pace.

"Grace—"

I hold up my hand. "She could be dead, Dad. How many more years are you going to live like she's still out there?"

Dad sits up a little straighter and swings his legs off the couch. He leans forward. "I know these last few years have been hard on you with all the moving around, but you can't give up hope. If they find her, they'll put her in the system. They'll notify us. It's just a matter of time."

The months have turned to years and the years have collected over a decade. The more time that passes, the more I know she will never be found.

"Dad, I've washed your coffee mug more times than I've seen you." I add under my breath, "It's not fair."

Dad stands up and holds out his hands to me, pleading, "I'm sorry, Grace. It's *not* fair. I know I'm not around as much as I should be. But we are so close to getting a handle on this disease."

I cross my arms. "You've said that every time they find a new marker gene. Every time they have a new drug that's supposed to be the miracle cure. Every time you have a lead on a new and even better doctor."

"What would you have me do then? Give up on her? On us as a family?"

"When have we been a family? It has been over a decade. Do you realize that?"

Dad shakes his head. "We have to keep trying."

I snort, "What happened to living instead of waiting for the next trial or the next discovery?"

"I can't just pretend she's dead, Grace. If there is even a minute chance she is alive . . ."

I throw up my hands, unable to contain my frustration. "Stop it, Dad! This isn't some ridiculous fairy tale. This is life. There is no cure and she isn't coming back."

Heavy lines of anger harden around Dad's mouth. He walks over to the woodstove and places his hands on the mantel, gazing up at the photo. He stares up at the two of them, so much in love when they first met all those years ago. He has worshipped here in front of this photo so many times that the rug beneath it has grown prematurely threadbare. Except I know that he doesn't believe in a god. He believes in science. He believes in the idea that humans can unlock the infinite capacities of our minds.

Dad turns and faces me, his voice firm and uncompromising, the way I have heard him speak when he is lobbying for more money to entice another doctor. "We don't know that, Grace. What the future holds. Not one of us can know that."

I want to scream that we do know. I know. And I would rather tear the flesh from my body before living that way. Before I say things that I will regret, I press my lips together and study the pattern on the rug.

"Gracie, I don't know what to tell you. I can't, I just can't let her go. If I didn't do everything in my power, how could I live with myself?" Dad steps forward with tears in his eyes. "Please, bugaboo, please. Your mother, she is my fairy tale. When we had you, that was my dream. She is with me every day, even if I can't touch her. Working on the next treatment, finding out as much as possible about the disease, it's the only way I know to bring her back. I'm doing this for us. For you."

I slump into myself. I know all this. Know that he will never stop until there is a cure or he dies trying. The one thing my father harbored in all his years in foster care was the insane belief that there could be a love to transcend all boundaries, all limits. He found that with my mother, and he has never let go.

So I tell him. "Dr. Mendelson believes they found a universal marker. SIC-5 affects the risk of a cluster of genes."

Dad freezes. "Is she sure?"

"She called it the Rosetta Stone."

"They are going to develop a test like Huntington's," he says quietly.

I stay silent.

I don't agree with Dad about the need to know. Why would anyone want to test for a gene like Huntington's disease just so they can look forward to their balance slowly eroding, followed by jerking limbs and deep depression, until finally they sink into madness and die prematurely? What is the point in learning how many repetitions are on chromosome four? So you can live out the rest of your life like one long bucket list? My only reason for knowing would be so that I could end it before it happened. So many years have passed since the discovery of the Huntington's gene, and still, there is no cure.

"It's the first step," Dad says as though reading my mind.

"First step to what?" I protest. "To killing yourself because you know you're just going to go crazy or wander the streets homeless or sit drooling in a hospital? All the wonderful amazing choices you have once you know you are fucked for life."

The clattering of train tracks rings for a moment and I turn my head toward the window.

Dad stares at me, shaking his head. "Grace, that's not true."

"Love doesn't conquer everything. It's all a stupid story."

"Don't say that, Grace."

"YOU DON'T UNDERSTAND!" I shout. "All this wasted time. Who's the crazy one for believing any of this can change?" The train whistles long and loud. I cover my ears and shrink back.

"Grace!"

The grinding of metal on metal pierces the room. The roar pounds on my mind.

"Nothing is going to make it better," I shriek into the oncoming train. "NOTHING!"

I am screaming so hard, Dad's face begins to fade. I can't stop. I can't stop. Dad begins to grow lighter, blending into the background of the room as the train draws closer and all I can do is clamp my hands over my ears before falling to the ground. I try to pound the noise out of my head.

My teeth sink into the soft flesh of my tongue. Blood pools in my mouth. I gag. Choke for air. My hands tremble against my lips. Scarlet drops fall to the floor.

"Dad!" I cry in fear. "Help me!"

How can there be a train? There is no train. This is not real. This is not real. I bury my hands into the rug. Grip every single fiber. But I hear it. Hear it coming for me. Feel the rumble beneath my feet. I will myself to die before the train explodes into the house. I smash my face against the floor. My nose fills with blood. The iron salt warmth pours down the back of my throat and chokes me. I curl into myself, pulling my knees up to my chest.

"Let me die," I whisper. Please. Let me die. I refuse to live like this. In this place.

I stop breathing.

Winter Spring Summer Autumn

You will command yourself to stop breathing as you study every line in the ceiling. Every scuff on the linoleum floor. In this place of barred windows and white ghostly figures rushing back and forth down halls, disappearing behind doors while other ghosts sit and scream at nothing and everything. The high-pitched shrill scream of a rusty wheel turning over and over in futility as the wheelchair moves past you making your skin crawl with pain.

Stop breathing. Stop it. But your body will betray you. Your lungs will fill with air. Your heart will continue to beat. You will feel the blood moving inside you, living. Living a life that will not be yours. In a body you will not want.

What other choice will you have after they assign you

to a room? Demand you go to art class for an outlet? You will wander the halls, listening to the voices all around you. Talking to you. At you. Inside you. Until you find a corner with a chair that no one else wants. Find a corner that is yours and when someone else sits there, you will shriek. Uncontrollably, inconsolably, your body arched violently backward until they slam a needle into the flesh that you try to tear off.

What will you do once the door of your room is closed shut? Your wrists and ankles restrained to the bed. What will happen as the chemicals begin to choke your thoughts and all you know is that little patch of sky in the high window? How inhumane, how cruel to show any signs of the outside world, and yet you will be thankful every day that you can stare out. Into the porthole of life illuminated hard and blue by a sun you cannot see or feel. What time? What month? You would willingly trade your soul and body just to know the season. As you lie alone, you will think you can see the flecks of the year's first snow. You will open your mouth to the birth of these sweet cold drops, only to find them turning to blood on your tongue. And in the final seconds before sleep steals your mind. Not conscious. Not unconscious. Not life. Not death. This suspended place and moment. Where snow tastes of blood. What will you do in this middle place?

This place that reeks of urine and bleach, iron, and fermenting bodies. This middle place. So heavy. So ripe. With despair.

Spring

The silence hunches over me in my dreams, a phantom heavy on my chest. The taste of blood is thick in my mouth. The gum-tight feel of it on my face. A confusion of memories crowds into my mind as I open my eyes, my back aching from being curled into a shivering ball on the floor. I stare at the photographs above the mantel, mocking me. Stupid girl. Stupid crazy girl. Just like your mother. I sit up slowly and gingerly touch the dried, caked blood under my nose. Outside, the clouds are just beginning to streak with the first red and orange of the rising sun. Miraculously, the sun splits open the sky to another day. Streaks of orange and crimson red and then high above, the stars still flickering, but in between are all the shades. Blue pierces my heart.

The breaking horizon is the color of my father's eyes. The last time he opened them before he died. All his life, he had called them hazel. Said they changed with the times, the seasons, the clothes he wore, the mood he was in. But the last time he opened his eyes to look at me sitting by his hospital bed, the last time, they were the blue of heavens and oceans. Forget-me-nots. And then he left me. Alone. Holding only a broken promise to always be there for me. He left me an orphan.

I rock back and forth, holding myself. Dad, I miss you. I miss you so much. I don't want to live anymore, Daddy. I can't live anymore. I don't know how to live anymore. Without you.

The shadows move across the floor. How long have I been sitting on the floor, watching the day open and pass? I begin to hear Dad moving in the kitchen. Telling me how the next round of trials will make significant changes for patients. For sufferers. How he has a new trail on Mom. Some grainy video of a woman buying a bus ticket and then causing a scene in the terminal. He says I need to work harder at the lab to give him more leads so that he can work on his next round of hires. I listen to him, but I refuse to join him in the kitchen. Instead I stay in my spot, hugging my knees to my chest and watching the light creep through the room. There is a pile of unopened bills on the floor in front of the mail slot next to the door, which I will only pay when they leave messages threatening to cut off the power. Somehow being eighteen means you are prepared to take care of a house, yourself, and the future. After the social worker stopped checking in because there was nothing more she could do, after all of Dad's coworkers stopped calling when I refused to talk, after everyone expected that I was better, I was left to do what all adults are supposed to do. Live. As though that was the solution to everything.

The phone rings. I stare at it, unsure of whether it is really ringing. I'm afraid to find out the truth. After it stops ringing, I pick it up and listen to the dial tone. I place it back on the cradle, and it immediately begins to ring again. Dad comes to the doorway and stares at me.

I pick it up.

"Hey, Grace. It's me, Will."

"Will?"

"You didn't show up at the lab this afternoon, so I thought I would check in. You know, make sure you made it home okay."

"I'm home."

"Yeah, I know," he says, and clears his throat. "You coming in today?"

"What time is it?"

"Four."

I listen for Dad in the kitchen, but he is gone. "I don't know."

"I could come pick you up if you—"

"No."

"It's not a problem, Grace. I remember where you live."

"What? How?"

"Remember your dad had me over for dinner? I think you had some kind of school thing. . . ."

"Yeah, I stopped coming to those dinners as soon as I got my license. There was always some after-school thing I could go to. Sometimes I even just sat on the side of the road watching the cars pass. Anything to stay out of the house." I remember all those dinners with the new recruits. The way Dad always needed to show them photos of Mama and me. How much all their work meant on a personal level. That was Dad. Making sure they knew what they were fighting for. Her. Him. Us. The love story.

"You must have hated hearing the same stories."

I glance up at the photos. "No, not really. I loved the stories. I just couldn't take the sad look in their eyes when Dad had such hope in his. But he never saw that, because he was too lost in all his hoping. . . ."

I don't want to talk about the relentless crushing weight of a bird clipped flightless, its beak an open maw needing to be fed and fed and fed. Even in the face of a reality clear as an open vein, my father refused to see it, with each day, which collected into months, then years, as the hemorrhaging continued, and she was not found, the location of the gene was not found, the cure was not found. After over a decade of searching, researching, testing—the finite limits of our bodies and minds must yield at some point.

Life does not exist without death. But "hopeless" was not in his vocabulary.

I look around at this empty house that was supposed to be a home for us. When she returned and we could be whole again. But it is not her or her ghost that returns, but my father. My father and his hoping filling my thoughts until I, too, cannot see, cannot hear, cannot feel where the mind ends and the fabric of this world begins.

"Grace?"

"What?"

"Grace, are you okay?"

"I'm fine," I snap. But as soon as I say the words, it feels like we both know the truth. I start to pick at the dried blood on my face.

"All right," he says. "How about dinner tomorrow at the diner? We can walk over from the lab."

"I don't like to stay that late," I say. "You don't have to be nice to me because of my father."

"Who says I'm being nice to you just for him?"

I grip the phone harder. "Well then, what is it? Help the Orphan Day?"

"You know, Grace, maybe it's not all about you," he says quietly. "Maybe I *need* someone . . . someone to talk to about who I lost. You're not the only one who feels this. Maybe I need a friend."

The rawness in Will's voice summons such an ache in my heart. I curl forward to insulate the pain. There are no sounds of the train. No whispers, no footsteps upstairs.

Only the truth of the cobalt twilight filtering into the kitchen, illuminating the two chairs at the kitchen table, one still tucked into place from the last time social services came by to check and see how I was managing on my own. I see the two mugs of coffee sitting on the counter from yesterday. Every morning I pour him a fresh cup. Every night I throw it out before I go to bed.

I can see the ghost of me moving through the kitchen. Every day. Existing. Leaning against the counter. Standing. Staring out the window. If I close my eyes and listen, really listen, Dad will return to me. He will come back to me. I trace the noises of the house. Where is he? The slow leak in the upstairs bathtub faucet. The monotone hum of the refrigerator.

"Grace?"

"Grace, let's have some soup."

"I have to go, Will." I slowly lower the phone to its cradle and then look up.

Dad leans forward, his hands gripping the edge of the doorway to the kitchen. The rectangular frame like a photo, opens a door into a place when he was always there for me.

WinterSpringSummerAutumn

She stood next to the swinging door, glaring back at the empty kitchen. She resisted pushing into the dining room. Instead, alone with her anger, she quickly ran back to the table and took the muffin from the plate and threw it on the floor. She began to dig her heel into the lying thing full of metallic sting instead of the sweetness and warmth she so craved.

In a minute the door swung open and Mama entered with a hurried air. She reached into the cabinet for a glass and then opened the refrigerator. She moved around the kitchen, pulling out the milk and pouring it into the glass. Where the back of her mother's shirt had once been neatly tucked in, it was now undone. The strange disorder of the line unnerved her. Mama set the glass of milk on the table.

"What did you do to the muffin? I can't understand what has gotten into you today," Mama said, and bent down to gather the larger pieces off the floor.

Gulp after cool gulp of milk finally washed away the salt. Her father entered the kitchen and walked over to the stove. Before she could warn him, he took a muffin from the tin and bit down.

She saw him gag before throwing the entire thing into the trash.

Mama turned around and saw him wiping his mouth.

"It's good," he choked out before walking over and taking her glass of milk to wash out the taste.

"It is?" Mama asked.

Dad smiled too happily for such a disturbing event. "I have to grab some paperwork, but then I'll be right back," he said, and leaned in, kissing Mama below her ear.

"Come here, bug." Dad leaned down and placed his forehead on hers, smiling into her eyes. He tapped her nose three times, quickly, their silent signal for the words *I love you.* All the sadness over the muffins disappeared with Daddy's touch.

"Why do you have to leave?" she asked. "Why can't you just stay?"

"I will be right back. So fast you won't even miss me."

"That is not the truth." She scowled. "I know how many minutes it takes for you to drive to the lab and back."

Daddy grinned at her. "You do? How many?"

"Thirty-three minutes without any traffic and much longer if there are cars on the road."

"How did you get so smart?"

She remained scowling.

Dad placed the palm of his hand on top of her head. "I promise when I get back, we can take a walk to the playground. Then get pizza for dinner and—"

"Ice cream cones afterward?"

"Yes, my love. I promise you ice cream and rainbows and all the stars in the sky. I promise I'm going to make everything perfect for you."

"Okay," she said, holding out her pinkie. "Remember what you promised."

He linked his pinkie with hers and then he was gone. The sudden absence of him left her confused. She thought about running out to the car and making him stay. She would gladly give up the playground, pizza, and ice cream if he would just stay. But she knew he would probably tell her she was being Unreasonable. Parents used that word a lot when they didn't want to do what you wanted.

She watched the door for a second more, hoping against hope that he would return magically, but when he did not, she turned back to her mother, who was crouching on the floor and picking up the rest of the crumbs from the smashed muffin.

"You asked me to make these for you all morning, and then this is what you do."

She thought of Daddy and his promises and stayed

silent as Mama chastised her for being ungrateful and threw the remnants of her poor behavior into the trash. Mama walked over to the stove and unconsciously reached over, breaking off a piece of another muffin and placing it in her mouth.

She rushed to the sink and spat. With her head lowered, her hands gripped the edge of the counter. Then slowly Mama straightened up and the heel of her palm rose up, pressed into the side of her head. She stood there, still and silent, the shadow of her raised arm cutting across the floor.

She stared over Mama's shoulder at the window, where the wind was whipping back the trees, their once-straight frames cowering and hunching over. The sky darkened. And then tiny white dots floated through the air. Right before her eyes, they proliferated, flooding the window until all that remained was white. A snow globe's swirling fantasy.

Mama screamed.

The violence of the cry, hard as a kick to the gut, made her jump in fear. She raised her knuckles to her mouth and stared at her shrieking mother.

Mama leaned forward, bending at the waist, hands on her knees. She screamed again. A howl so deep it seemed to crawl across the floor like a wild animal clawing its way to bite her.

She stepped back.

Then Mama was all motion, arms flailing as she threw

muffin after muffin into the trash. Some she smashed, fisting them in her hand before heaving them away. Mama swung her body back and forth, grabbing at anything, the muffin tin, the wooden spoon, the towels, the teakettle, anything within reach. Mama began to heave it all against the wall, the floor.

She began inching toward the door when Mama's eyes found her. Mama's eyes lasered into her and she could not move.

Winter **Spring** Summer Autum

I'm frozen in my place at the sink, my reflection in the window directly before me. Behind me, Dad moves through the kitchen, talking about tomato soup and a grilled cheese sandwich, which is just as good as pizza and how they are exactly the same except in a slightly different formulation. He rattles on, discussing the lab and how the new recruit is moving out here to work for Dr. Mendelson. The surfer wunderkind that Dad went to see in Australia. Sometimes our past conversations played over and over again in a Möbius strip.

I look into the darkness of the night transforming the window into a mirror and imagine what someone from the outside would see. A lone girl standing and staring into an empty field.

But inside, in the reflection, I see us the way we always were and will be. Locked in a place and time by the residue of life and the love that bound us. We were never orphans when we were together. Reflections are the illusions of what cannot be known from the outside.

Dad moves upstairs now, coughing hard as he gets ready for bed. The cough that lasted all winter is back again. I walk up the stairs to my bedroom and along the way pass the myriad of my school portraits. Missing upper teeth in that one, too-long bangs in another. Acne, brown corduroy jumper, spiked hair, pigtails, eyeliner. Thirteen portraits of a life frayed at the ends, bounded and boundless.

I climb a few more steps and stop at the picture of me when I was eight. My tight tiny smile as my brows gather in concentration. The heavy bangs cutting diagonally across my forehead. I remember this time so clearly. It was the first time that Dad and I had moved away from our house by the train tracks. Without their consistent presence reminding me of the time of day, evening, or night, I became anchorless.

I climb to the very top step and look behind me at the wall of memories. Who are we in the end? A collection of photos? How do we know what is truly lived if we cannot remember it? Dad holds on to the pictures like precious jewels. They are the first things that he unpacks. The first things he hangs on the walls before anything else is done to settle in. The pictures of the life we had so long ago. The only new pictures are the ones of me collecting an award, the odd holiday pose in front of the tree. Me in front of the sterile blue background of school portraits.

There are no pictures of Dad after Mama disappeared. The only pictures that remain are the ones in my mind: Dad reading medical studies, his sheepish look as he picks me up late again, the glow of the screen on his face as he researches online, the crook in his neck as he talks on the phone to scientists, detectives, hospital administrators, his joy at my first science-fair project winning regionals. The moments collect together and beat in my heart. Dad is still here. And if I cannot keep him alive, then I would rather we both be forgotten.

I begin to prepare for bed as I do every night. I will brush my teeth. I will wash my face. I will use the toilet one last time. After I enter the bathroom and stand before the mirror, I glance at my reflection and find a shadow looming behind me. When I whirl around, there is nothing there. After pacing the small space, opening drawers, searching for the shadow, which eludes me, I run back into my room and slam the door. I crawl into bed with my clothes on and pull the covers over my body, leaving the lights on in case the shadow returns. There was a shadow, I repeat over and over. I saw the shadow. It was real. I saw it. It was real. I saw it. It was real. My eyes begin to drift closed. I saw it. It was real. I saw it.

The tomb of sleep finally descends.

Summer

You will die every night only to be reborn the next day. The marrow of your bones birthing cell after cell. Muscle covering skeleton. Flesh folding over muscle. Hair coating flesh. Lungs expanding.

Your eyes will open and you will look down at the body of someone living. A life that is filled with the death of you. Second by second. Minute by minute. Hour by hour. Time passing through you like a sieve. And then the siren songs will begin.

You will listen to the whispers. Light and sweet at first. You will welcome them with familiar thrills. Here is home. Here is your family. They welcome you. Join you. They have been waiting all this time. You will look at them and wonder where they went and how they came back. You will try to hold each of them in your arms. And when you can't, they will anger. Their voices changing to ash and coals. You were never happy with them. You left them. You were too weak to stop it. How could you let them disappear?

You will stand up to leave, but they will follow you. Pester and torment you. Words, simply words, you will say, but when the voices cannot be ignored, you will begin to sing. Softly to yourself at first. Then louder. Then screaming into the cave of your mind. Fighting and yelling at them to leave. You will slam your head against the wall over and over again to fight against their voices invading like skittering insects crawling through your skull.

You will see the nurse approaching, his hand clutching a small cup of pills. He grips your forearm. You will try to thrash out of his hands, but he will force the pills into your mouth. He will be stronger and hold his hand over your lips to keep you from spitting them out until all you can do is swallow. Swallow your life and voice and everything you should hate, but want and know this is how it is supposed to be.

When the voices leave, they part silently, disappearing one by one like melting snowflakes whispering, *Traitor.* Your family. You will weep, searching for them in the halls. Turning corner after corner only to sit down and realize you have never moved from your chair. Lost in the mirror halls of your mind. You will stand up crying. In grief. In love. With ghosts. In confusion. In pain. In heat. In cold. Inside. Outside. This skin burns. This skin is not yours. You will try and peel off what is not yours. Peel it off layer by layer with the nails that they cut to the quick. So you will use your teeth. Grab sections and peel it away to reveal what is underneath. The red of you. The meat of you. This is you. This will be the true you hiding under all the lies and voices. The trails of red that run down your body and spread across the white floor. The smear you will make with your fingers in the red pools collecting like rain on potholed streets. That will be you.

Winter Spring SummerAutum

The ruts in the road are beginning to fill with the slush of ice and water as the rain beats down relentlessly. I stand at the threshold of the open front door, smelling the air. It is of earth, damp hay, and dark attics, rising up through the foggy mists.

"Dad, your coffee's on the counter," I yell before I heave my backpack onto my shoulder and step out into the drizzling wetness.

"Thanks, bug," Dad calls. "I'm going to remember the pizza tonight. I promise."

The exhaustion I feel as I maneuver the Lincoln over the slippery road toward school almost makes me turn the car around and head home. I gingerly touch the bump on my nose. I don't think it's broken, but all the blood I had to scrub out of the rug makes me question my own diagnosis. At least I can breathe.

Suddenly the sun peeks out from behind a cloud and the bright light blinds me for a second. I blink quickly to keep the road ahead in sight. In the distance, a dark shape forms on the horizon. I wheeze and eagerly press on the gas. Hannah's figure looms ahead of me. She is walking.

"Hey," I say, and frantically wave as I pull up next to her.

She glances through the window and pauses. I stop the car completely and jump out.

"I don't want any more lectures," she says.

"I don't have any. Come on, Hannah. Please . . . I miss you."

Hannah smiles and my heart stills for a beat. Her brown eyes in that moment are so familiar to me. As though transported through time. The relief I feel at her forgiveness is immense. She is still my friend. And that knowledge means more than I could have imagined.

As soon as she is in the car, I am running my mouth about how there is a new guy at the lab and there is this hush-hush secret that I wish I could tell her about, but then I would have to cut off my tongue and possibly hers as well. She listens to all this without a single word but continues to smile at me through it all. I have truly missed her.

"Where have you been these last two weeks? You

haven't been at school. Did you go to Costa Rica with Dave?"

She absentmindedly nods as we pull into the school parking lot. A group of guys standing on the lawn, including Dave, watch us drive by. I maneuver the beast over to the far side of the lot to keep as much distance between Dave and Hannah as possible. I just want a few more minutes alone with her.

"Why do we have to park so far away?" she asks.

"Can we just catch up for a minute? I know you're gonna just go and be with Dave when we get into school."

Hannah shifts in her seat, and her long greasy hair falls into her face. I can smell that she hasn't showered in days. The veins in the back of her hands stand out like tunneling worms.

"Are you getting enough to eat?" I ask.

She shrugs. "Enough," she says quietly.

"Hannah, you can't keep going like this. Have you thought about what you want to do?"

Hannah remains silent, her hands folded neatly in her lap like she is at church. "I know how you feel about this, Grace."

"Remember I vowed lecture radio silence." I smile.

"I told him, and he wants me to have the baby."

I want to throw up my hands and ask if she is insane, but instead I nod and keep the fake smile Sharpied on my lips.

"I want a family, but is this just a cliché?" Hannah's eyes fill with tears. "Some teen mom bullshit?"

"Do you love him, Hannah?" I ask gently.

She looks away from me. "I don't know. I don't know about anything. What am I supposed to do after high school? Find a job? Go to college? I don't have the grades like you, Grace."

"You could go to a community college. Transfer later. Get a job for now and—"

"Stop! I don't have plans like that, Grace."

"It just sucks, Hannah. I wish you could see that you have so many options. Choices that you can't even know about in the future. Don't you want the freedom to see what happens?"

Hannah cups her slightly protruding belly. "This is all I have."

I lean forward, my neck stretching tight with all the things I want to say, but instead I tell her a truth. "I wish my mom and dad never had me. If I could have had a say in all of it, I would have said no."

Hannah turns away from me. Immediately, the horrible meaning of my words sinks between us. I reach out, but she flinches away.

"I'm so sorry," I say. "I didn't meant that. I know I said I wouldn't do this. Please, Hannah," I beg, "please, don't be mad at me. I can't sleep. I'm just tired and cranky."

Hannah nods but won't look up at me. She dashes away the tears with the back of her hand and then opens the door to step out. As we walk away from the car, my throat raw from the scraping words, I wonder about what choices we really do have in life. What did my mother and father know of love? Of bringing me into a world and a life that was never going to be truly mine?

If I had known that one day my father would crucify himself all for a childhood dream . . . if I had known that I would have a runaway mother lost inside her own locked mind, forever in a world within a world . . . what choices do we really have in this life?

In the distance, walking toward us, I see a lone guy. Hannah instantly turns to me. "Don't start anything, Grace."

"Can I just talk to him, Hannah? Please? I just want to ask him if he is really going to take care of you."

She studies the ground for a second and then nods before walking back to the car.

Dave stops in front of me. He shuffles his feet for a second and hoists his backpack higher up on his shoulder. Without his posse of friends, he looks, and acts, naked.

He casts his eyes over my shoulder to the car. I step forward to block his view.

"Hey, Dave, can we talk?"

"Yeah. Sure."

"Do you really know what you are doing?"

"You know, Grace, I might be messed up about a lot of stuff, but I wasn't raised to just cut and leave. My faith means a lot to me. I want to do the right thing."

"What way were you raised?" I snap back.

"Cut me some slack, Grace. You're always so angry.

Can't people make a mistake and then try and make up for it?"

"So it was all just one big mistake!"

"That's not what I meant! This baby—"

"Stop calling it a baby. It's a group of cells. A zygote."

"That is your scientific bullshit."

"There is a reason your GOD gave scientists the brains to create birth control and abortion. The reason why women have the right to choose. Thank God he's merciful."

"I don't know why I'm even trying to talk to you." He shoves his hands into his pocket and turns to leave, but then changes his mind. "I actually prayed on this, Grace. I'm not a bad guy. I mean, look at all those people who can't have babies. What's wrong with adoption?"

I gape at him. "Seriously? All because of your precious religious beliefs you want the woman to carry and birth your child while you party and vomit and fuck your way through college?"

Dave lowers his voice. "That's not what I'm saying. Stop twisting my words. I made a stupid mistake. I have to deal with it too, you know."

"Wow, you really are dealing with everything."

"I'm not ready to be a father, Grace. I'm not ready to do that for anyone."

Lies. All his lies. And Hannah crying and waiting for him to be her fairy tale. I push his chest hard with both hands. "Asshole!"

He grabs my wrist and yanks me away from him.

I reach up and grab him by the hair. Bite his shoulder.

"Get off me!" He pushes me away.

I run at him again, grabbing one sleeve of his jacket and tearing at it. I refuse to let go even as he tries to twist away. My breath heaves and my heart races as a distant clanking noise of the train rattles me. No, I can't let him see me this way. The train is coming. I lunge and hit as hard as I can.

"STOP!" He throws me to the ground.

The back of my head slams against the pavement. Silence screams.

In dead silence, Mama dashed across the room and grabbed her by the waist, pulling her down and under the kitchen table. Together they kneeled, hunched over, tented by the tablecloth from the outside world. Mama stared at the floor.

She wanted Mama to stop acting so strange, like a sleepwalker in the sun. She reached out slowly, her fingertips brushing skin. Mama startled at her touch.

"Mama, why are you so quiet?" she asked softly.

Mama glanced at her.

"I hear it," Mama said in a whisper.

Under the table, with the drape of the tablecloth partly obscuring their view, it felt as though they could be camping. Or pretending that they were in a fort together. Protected from all intruders. She leaned into Mama.

"Let's pretend they can't find us under here, Mama. Like Frog and Toad," she said.

Mama nodded. "We are safe under here, aren't we?"

"Yes," she said. "Remember our spell?"

Mama smiled. Sometimes they did that when she had been younger and afraid of the dreams. The dreams that wound their way into her nights and she awoke crying. The three of them sat on her bed and said spells to ward off the bad dreams.

"Mist and light. Darkness bright. Shield us from the evil fright."

Mama repeated the words, "Mist and light. Darkness bright. Shield us from the evil fright."

Mama's hands were clenched, her face sweaty and tight with fear. Over and over they repeated their spell. But still Mama would not stop her trembling. Mama began to mutter other words. "Father, Father. God, hear me. This will not end here. Please, Father. Please, I cannot. I beg you. Father. God. Father. Lord. I beg you. Please do not ask this of me." Mama knitted her hands together so hard the skin of her fingers turned red and white.

She did not know what to do when Mama went inward like this. She remembered her father holding his hand over her mother's lips once when Mama would not, could not stop screaming. He had shoved the pills that she refused to take into her mouth. Made her swallow them.

"Mama, you need your pills," she whispered. "I'll go get them." She began to edge out from under the table. "Don't worry, I'll be right back."

"NO!" Mama shrieked, and grabbed her arm. "No, you cannot leave. You'll die if you leave."

Mama locked eyes with her, and she spoke so low it sounded more like a snarl than words. "The train is coming for us. Listen."

She strained to listen for the train. All she could hear was the sunlight dappling the floors.

Winter **Spring** SummerAutum

I squint against the glaring sun before slowly propping myself up.

Dave stands off to the side, his eyes tight with confusion and fear. He holds his backpack close to his chest as though shielding himself. "You really are crazy," he shouts. "What is wrong with you? You need help." He turns around and heads quickly back to the school buildings.

A white plume streaks through the blue sky as a jet races up toward the heavens. A moment later a deep rumble thrums and beats down on me. Hannah crouches beside me, her hair falling into her face. I sit up. Gingerly, my fingertips trace the swelling bump on the back of my head.

"Grace, are you okay?" Hannah whispers.

"I'm sorry, Hannah," I say. "He said the worst shit—I couldn't control myself. . . ."

"What did he say?"

"He said something about faith and adoption or some kind of bullshit."

Hannah's lips press together, her face draining of color. "Adoption."

I let out a deep breath. "Hannah, you can do anything. This is your body. This is your decision."

She tucks a strand of her hair behind her ear and looks away from me toward the woods. She stands up and I follow after.

"I have to get away from here." Her hands wander over her belly.

"Do you want me to come with you?" I ask. "I don't want you to be alone like this."

"Thanks, Grace." Hannah smiles at me and I know all has been forgiven. "I just need to be alone right now."

I watch Hannah cut into the woods and then disappear from view. I head toward the only place that I know makes sense, even if it feels like jail most of the time.

Driving to work in the afternoon, the comforting thought of performing mindless duties, which will keep my mind off the fight with Dave and the look on Hannah's face before she turned away, unknots the tension in my shoulders. I ache for the numbers that will soothe me.

At Genentium, when the glass doors close with a quiet shush behind me, I stand for a second in my place and savor the peace. I know who I am here. Walking through security, taking the elevators down to level B4, even gazing at the numbers illuminated on the elevator panel bring me comfort.

I check the bulletin board as soon as I walk into the lab to see what duties I have been assigned. Next to my name, instead of instructions, I find a sheet folded in half with my name on the front. A thumbtack lances it closed. I take it down and open it up to find a time and name scribbled inside. Why does Dr. Mendelson want to see me? I check the clock. Fifteen minutes until the meeting. This I do not know how to process.

I run to the nearest bathroom and lock myself in a stall. Shit, what does Dr. Mendelson want with me? Pacing in a tight circle, I tell myself to get it together. Don't go crazy now, Grace. I check my watch. Shit. I race out of the stall and run over to the sink to check my appearance in the mirror. For the first time in what feels like forever, the reflection of my face emerges crystal clear—my strange bloated features and dark circles under my eyes. Turning from side to side, I see a large matted section of oily hair and I slowly work it with my fingers, combing through the knot as best as I can. When was the last time I brushed it? A memory of Mama, her disheveled clothes and greasy hair, flits through my mind. I think about all the cans of soup filling the recycling bin. The few pizza boxes and odd to-go containers mixed in. The nasty food has been taking a toll. I run some water over my hands and pat down my hair as best I can. I tuck in a stray strand behind my ears.

At the door to Dr. Mendelson's office, which is closed and, unlike all the other doors in the lab, made of solid wood instead of opaque glass per her instructions, I knock twice.

Her muffled voice calls out, "Come in."

I turn the knob and walk into her office.

"Hello, Grace," Dr. Mendelson says without looking away from her computer screen. "Have a seat."

I carefully sit down at one of the two leather chairs arranged in front of her desk. Dr. Mendelson quickly types and then her fingers pause. She glances over at me before her fingers resume working until she finally pushes the keyboard away.

"Thanks for coming to see me at such short notice. I hope I haven't pulled you away from anything too critical."

I stare at her face, wondering if she is joking or being serious. Would sterilizing beakers be considered critical work? I think I know the answer to this one. I shake my head no.

She abruptly stands and comes over to the other leather chair, sitting down beside me before I even have a chance to shift my body around from facing her desk.

"Grace, I want to apologize for not checking in on you more since your father's passing." She angles closer and I begin to worry that she might reach for my hand.

I cross my arms and hide my hands. "I've been doing fine."

"As you know, the pacing has ramped up since we were approved for the clinical trials this summer."

I nod.

She pauses for a moment and kneads the back of her neck with one hand. "And I suppose I believed somehow that to really honor your father was to do the work that he wanted most. We have been searching for this universal marker for a very long time."

I nod again.

She reaches out for my hand and when she can't find it, she reaches over and pats my knee. "But that doesn't take the place of really making sure to check in on you. I know your father had some very personal reasons for wanting this research to move forward."

She is talking to me, but all I can think about is the feel of her hand on my knee.

"Grace?"

I look up. "Yes?"

"I was just asking if you have heard anything about your application to Yale."

Her words blaze through the fog in my head and the image of the e-mail that I flagged but never bothered to read comes to mind. I never told her I applied early to only one school. I stopped caring or remembering at some point. I shake my head no.

She pats my knee again. "Well, I'm sure they'll be contacting you shortly. A girl with your potential. They would be fools not to accept you."

I force myself to say the right things instead of letting my mind go down the rabbit hole of emotion. "Thank you for taking the time to write that recommendation. I know how busy you are."

"Grace, it was the very least I could have done."

From the corner of my eyes, I see a slight bulging of the floor. I lower my hands to my thighs and pinch the flesh as hard as I can. Keep it together. Small black spiders edge into my vision.

". . . I want to be frank with you about your progress here at the lab . . ."

I feel them crawling over my ankles and knees. I stand up.

"Grace, are you okay?"

I look around the room. The spiders are gone.

"Grace."

I feel a tap on my shoulder.

I turn around. "Dr. Mendelson—sorry, I just got dizzy for a second." I sit back down in my chair.

"I'm worried about you, Grace. You seem anxious lately. Are you faring all right in that big house on your own?"

"Yes, I'm fine. I have midterms, so I've been hitting those books," I say, hoping to sound like a normal high schooler.

Dr. Mendelson stands up and walks quickly behind her

desk, but she doesn't sit. She shifts her weight back and forth from the balls to the heels of her feet as she studies me, her eyes a CAT scan moving up and down.

I wait quietly until she finally stops rocking.

"You are not alone, Grace. I know it can feel that way when you are under all the stress of grief, but we are here for you just like the way your father championed for so many of us at Genentium."

I press my lips together as a spike of anger slides between my ribs. I am not in mourning. Dr. Mendelson sees my expression and clears her throat.

"I called you in here to talk about your January report about chromosome twenty-two, Grace. Did that come directly from you and not something you heard from another scientist, perhaps? Did you ever inadvertently take some paperwork home or show it to anyone else? Dr. Diaz, your supervising scientist, told me that you had asked her to look further at the data."

I run both my hands over my face. My mind slowly computes her questions. Is she wondering if I somehow pilfered data from another scientist? What is she asking me?

"Grace . . ."

I lean forward. "I would never take data out of this lab, Doctor. Nor did I work with any other scientist in this lab on work that was specifically assigned to me. I know the rules. I submitted the report based on my own findings."

"Then Grace, tell me why you asked Dr. Diaz to take

a closer look at chromosome twenty-two and in particular the absences."

I pause before I try to explain, glancing quickly at the floor, which remains flat and shiny as polished wood. I look up and find Dr. Mendelson waiting for my answer.

My knowledge of genetics and science is absolutely zero compared to Dr. Mendelson or Dr. Diaz, but I do know numbers. Have always known numbers.

"When I was inputting the data . . . I started to see . . . the results didn't make sense. I began to rearrange the figures in my head and—" I pause. There is no way that I can explain how I see numbers floating in space, arranging themselves in the air. Twisting and turning like leaves in the wind until they string together like Christmas tree lights, twinkling and shining so bright that the darkness of the hole, the omission, is too dark to ignore. This is not something anyone would believe, so I keep it simple. "I saw an omission. It didn't make sense."

Dr. Mendelson nods, encouraging me to continue.

"I thought I had inputted some data incorrectly, and as I was trying to go back and fix the errors, I noticed a few other errors. But then when I was double-checking the inputs, I saw that they weren't errors, but rather omissions. The program wasn't picking up on it because it was looking for repeats on the chromosomes, so I asked Dr. Diaz to double-check my theory."

It all sounds so implausible even to my ears. How could an intern see something that a sophisticated program or even the leading scientists couldn't see?

"Grace." Dr. Mendelson sits down next to me. "I would like to move you over to my team."

I sit back in shock.

Dr. Mendelson leans forward. "I take it from your expression that you weren't quite expecting that."

I shake my head. "But I haven't even graduated from high school," I stammer.

"Yes, I am aware of that," she says. "I like to believe in omens. And Grace, you are going to bring some good luck to my lab."

"But you're a scientist. How can you believe in luck and omens?"

A slight rise in the corner of Dr. Mendelson's lip is about as close to an expression of happiness as I have ever seen. "Oh Grace, have you not seen how much of our work is nothing but religion? Our place of worship is here. Our scriptures and prophets are the texts and scientists who have come before us. We are just as adamant and at times fanatical as any zealot."

"No," I protest. "Science is proven. We have results that we check over and over again. We see the way people can change when we develop drugs to help combat the illness. Fevers go down after taking aspirin. These are facts."

"And what of the Tibetan monks raising their core temperatures while meditating? Is this also not a fact? Have miracles not been proven? Science is but the path we have chosen to understand what we do not know."

I look away. And what about what we do know? What we can't fix? What has always been, for generations over lifetimes? Where do the threads of this life end and where do they begin? Or is it just an endless tangle? A DNA strand?

"Grace, what is faith but the belief in your chosen religion? What is faith but blind hope? Do you have faith in science? History? How many times has it all been proven wrong?"

"I don't know," I say. And for the first time, I wonder if my father's relentless need to find answers, a cure, treatments to bring her back has been his form of religion. I just never believed the way he did.

"Neither do I. I don't have the answers. Which is why I also believe you will be a valuable asset to my team."

Once she stands up, I do the same. She places an arm around my shoulder and leads me to the door. "Your father would be very proud of you, Grace."

I walk out of Dr. Mendelson's office and into the long, empty hallway. With each footfall, the echo of my presence seems to radiate all around me. The sound floats around me like phantoms. When I look back, the hallway lengthens and stretches as though I have walked a thousand miles along a corridor that leads nowhere. My mind throbs, unbalancing me. No, no, not here, I beg. I walk forward and focus on the doors of the labs. Count them in my head as I pass . . . five, six, seven. A faint high-pitched whistle skitters into my ears. The growing crescendo of metal grinding against metal makes me stop and reach for the wall with both hands to steady myself. My eyes close against everything I do not want to see.

There is a bridge on which I stand. Behind me, all the years of my life shimmer and pulse. I remember the smooth weight of my mother's hair like cradling threads of black gold in my hands. Dad reading to me in front of the woodstove as the heat burns into the heels of my outstretched feet. Running to the edge of the ocean as the moist salt spray coats my lips. All these moments of living in a place where water and earth and air come together precisely forming the present, a break line of space and time between past and future where life moves and struggles, rages and crawls, dances, calms, naps with arms thrown wide open, touching other lives, inhaling their scent, their breath. This existence will no longer be mine.

Ahead of me, I see the shadow of the train approaching. The thundering echoes grow louder and louder, pulling me forward into a life that is not of my making. The helix of time will swirl around and through me until I am no longer alive, but existing in a place between breaths. I stand on the bridge of prodrome, mourning all that will be lost and all that is to come. I stand on this bridge, waiting for the train. Waiting to fall backward.

Unless . . .

I jump.

Winter SpringSummerAutumn

The Fates. I remember you were always bringing up the Fates. The Fates like layers of reality stacked high as reams of paper handed over to you, biblical in totality. The Fates were no minor gods, you always argued.

I disagreed and always tried to make you understand my views. So what was the point of life then? What choices are truly our own versus what has been handed down through your Fates? This existence. This body. Who says this is reality or just a version of some cyborg dream? A wormhole into another consciousness? How do we begin to understand where, why, and how we live? The idea that only one truth can exist is not a truth, I argued. Fates have been known to change. With faith.

How is it that your smile was always so gentle, as though gazing upon a petulant child?

What is faith? you asked. A feeling? A premonition? A belief in the face of despair, above will and exertion? Faith is not wanting to know what is true.

Stop quoting Nietzsche, that fascist elitist. Faith is as air, love, fire, hunger, hope. Faith is elemental.

That is not on the periodic table, you said, and walked away.

Always, always you had your Fates. The tests that foretold your future. And no matter how much I tried, I could never convince you to believe that it could be different with faith. But I tried. I tried to convince you until the day you left. And even after you had gone, I kept my faith. For living in this version of reality was not a reality that I would accept as the truth.

Winter Spring SummerAutumn

I am willing away the rattle of the tracks. Staring at the smooth concrete floor of the hall, telling my mind what I know and see before me. There is no train.

"Grace?"

I look up. "Do you hear it?"

"Hear what?" Will asks.

I take a breath to explain, but the words won't come. Will stands before me, slowly reaches out his hand.

In one breathless moment, I stretch as far as I can, the tendons and muscles of my arm and hand contracting in pain. I grab hold before I fall.

"I hear something," I whisper. "There is a train. I hear a train. Listen."

Will guides me gently to a door and then another door and then around a corner. Somewhere between all the twists and turns of entering and exiting labs and rooms, I lose sight of where I am and where I am going. I can only feel the gentle pressure of Will's hands on the roundness of my shoulders.

And then I am alone. Sitting on a couch facing a wall of caged animals. I gaze around the strange room, unable to comprehend if we are still in the lab. The soft yellow lights on the mice, rats, primates, and rabbits make this place seem more like a pet store. Trying to shake myself out of it, I remind myself that this *is* the lab. These are test subjects. I study the movements of all these lives trapped behind their clear plastic cages. Each so alone and yet joined in their suffering and purpose.

The soft scurrying noise of the rodents and the warmth of the room envelop me. While I know intellectually that this is a torture chamber, being faced with their lives brings me comfort for some reason. Maybe it's the knowledge that I am not the only one in pain. I sink back into the couch, watching these little creatures busy in their work. Sleeping curled in corners. Chewing wood shavings. Clutching water bottles. Pressing paws to cage wall, sniffing at the air that has been disturbed by my presence.

Will appears from behind a door with a glass of water. He sits down next to me and offers me the drink.

"Grace, has the train stopped?"

I listen carefully. "Yes." I turn away, embarrassed that he

has heard my confusion. My confession. "I feel so stupid. It was probably just a piece of equipment."

"Don't be embarrassed. We all have those moments of dislocation."

I take a sip of water. The coolness slips down my throat and clarity begins to emerge again. Will leans forward and places his elbows on his knees, hands clasped in front of him.

"Remember when I said I wanted to tell you about my life?"

I nod and focus on steadying the glass of water in my hands.

"I have, or I should say, I had, a twin sister. She was my best friend."

"I'm so sorry," I whisper.

He shrugs. "Thanks." He looks at me. "You know, we were so alike we even both surfed goofy." He notes my expression. "That just means we surfed with our right foot forward."

I force myself to smile.

"She was my better self. In all ways. Older, smarter, stronger, nicer, funnier, more popular. Although . . ." He frowns. "I contend that I was the better-looking twin."

"I bet that was debatable," I note.

"Hey, I had to claim something."

We both smile, and the moment of lightness feels so good we sit in silence and let it linger between us.

"You must miss her," I finally say.

"All the time."

"How long has it been since you lost her?"

"She died four years ago. She had schizophrenia."

I turn to stare at the animals; their noises seem louder. Will stands up and checks on one of the rats in the bottom row, who is making strange echoing squeaks.

"Was she in a hospital at the end?"

Will shakes his head and returns to the couch. "No, she was home with me and my parents. She was getting better. The medication was working. It felt like a miracle. I was so happy to have her back. It was almost like the way it had always been between us. I thought . . ." Will looks down at his hands. "I *thought* she was getting better. But then a few weeks later—"

The slight screeching sound of an exercise wheel turning and turning and turning fills the room.

"My dad has this sword collection. And . . . she got into the room."

I reach out and place my hand on Will's arm. "You don't have to tell me if this is hard."

"No, I *need* to talk about it. Otherwise, her death would have been pointless. Her life . . . can still help others. That's what I believe."

I nod and take my hand away from his arm.

"I found her with the sword and I tried to take it away from her." Will holds out his palms. "That's how I got these scars. But I got the sword away from her."

I reach out and gently trace the edges with my finger.

It must have been so painful, but he had not let go of the blade. My vision blurs as I think about how hard those who love us must work to save us.

"It didn't do any good, though. Because in the end, she still found a way to end her life a few days later." Will takes my hand in both of his, the rough ridges of his scars pressing into my skin. "You know what I want more than anything? I want answers. Why her and not me? What this sickness means. It makes no sense. Even a car accident I can understand. But to see someone lose their mind piece by piece, moment by moment. Why?"

"Why not?" I ask. "Are we supposed to be invincible? Isn't there always a price to be paid? We pillage our environment and we suffer natural disasters. The rich use the poor and we have riots. It's history, Will. Our human history. We have fucked-up diseases that pass on from generation to generation, repeating one too many genes or being completely absent on some random chromosome. It's not why, but when."

Will shakes his head. "No, I refuse to accept that. She was robbed of her life because of a disease that we can control. We are not invincible, but we can evolve."

I slip my hand from his and stare into his eyes. I tell him a truth. "I'm glad my mother disappeared."

Will exhales loudly.

"I'm glad because she scared me. I have lived a life free from that fear ever since. And I think . . ." I shake my head. "No, I know she was doing that for me. Dad never wanted to believe she was sane when she left that day. He thought it was her schizophrenia that made her leave us . . . him. That it wasn't her choice, which was why he had to find her. But how do you tell someone that you can't truly *find* a crazy person? I was the only one home with her the day she left."

The memory of that day, how she fell to her knees and pulled me so close, her nose sinking into my hair, moving to the crook of my neck as she inhaled so deeply it felt as though the essence of me was being pulled away . . . And then she stood up, placed the palm of her hand against my cheek, and said, "You are my life." I never saw her again except in the memories and dreams she left behind and the pictures that served as an altar for my father.

"And what I think is . . . that . . . in a moment of sanity, she left to spare us." A lightning bolt of pain shoots across my forehead. I grimace and press the heels of my palms against my temples.

"Are you okay? Grace, I'm worried about you."

I take a moment to breathe long and deep. The air catches in my throat for a second. The pain subsides. I lower my hands. "I'm fine," I say. "It's nothing."

Will studies me. "Grief makes life a magnificent challenge. I can see that in you. But I'm worried about—"

"You think I'm going crazy," I blurt out.

Will stammers, "N-no, it's not that. No, it's just you've changed so much. Even in the short time I've known you." But the blush rising up his neck tells me the truth.

"Just because my mom was crazy doesn't mean I'm going to follow in her footsteps. I'm just tired. I eat canned soup and pizza every day. I miss my father. I have a lot of work. My friend is having problems."

"Grace, slow down. No one is saying you're crazy."

"Good, because I'm not."

"But something's changed in you. When I found you in the diner, you didn't look like yourself. You actually looked like you were going to throw up."

My hands are shaking and the water sloshes back and forth in the glass. "I was really cold that night. I was walking for a while, thinking about my parents. What Dr. Mendelson announced would have meant the world to them. Before."

Will nods. "I know what you mean. I kept thinking of Sarah and what it would have been like if she had lived. The new drugs and the trials might have offered her a way to live as she wanted. Not the way she was forced."

"Is that why she killed herself?" After I ask the question out loud, I realize that I am hungry to know everything about her decision.

"No," Will says, and shakes his head. "No, Sarah was suffering from her disease. Sometimes I could see the part of Sarah that was still inside. The Sarah I always knew. But that part of her was so tangled in the voices and visions. Every once in a while, she would say something and it was like she had broken free. But it happened less and less. She got really quiet in the end." Will turns to me. "But she always smiled when she saw me. She always recognized me. I guess that was why I thought she was getting better."

"But she didn't die from the schizophrenia," I say gently. "She killed herself."

Will looks at me with an incredulous expression. "How is that different?"

"It was her choice."

"How is that a true choice when she's not even in control of her mind? The voices told her she wasn't worth it. They told her to do it. Maybe the voices were telling your mother to walk away."

"Or maybe she decided to do it when she was truly herself. You said you saw those glimmers underneath."

"Grace, I don't know where these questions are leading, but we thought the medication was working. What we didn't realize was . . . she had stopped taking them."

They love and hate their demons. Will sees the look in my eyes.

"I don't know what is worse," he continues. "Having so much hope only to have it crushed, or not to hope at all."

"If you're like my father, you hold on to hope until you die still gripping it with both hands." I think about his last words to me and I want to smash open every single cage, release every hopeless creature into the wild.

"Your father could convert anyone into a believer."

"Not everyone," I say, shaking my head. "Not me. You know, before my father died, his last words to me were about how the new recruit was going to make a big difference. There could be a discovery soon. My father is dying and all he can think about is the next cure, locating the gene. Not that he is leaving me. Not that I might *not* care about anything but a life without my father." Anger turns my voice haggard and ugly, but I can't stop. "Not that he loves me."

"But Grace, how could he have known that was the last time he would see you?"

I know what Will is trying to do.

"It doesn't matter. A part of him left when my mother left. I was just seeing the ghost of him most of the time anyway."

Will reaches out to touch my shoulder, but I jerk away and he lowers his hand. "Grace, he thought he was helping."

"He wanted a cure," I say. "He wanted her back. And even with all the best doctors … The hardest part is remembering when she was okay. I remember her. Being with her. Loving her as my mom. But then she was also someone else. Like a stranger living inside her body. She scared me."

"The drugs are so much better now, Grace."

"God, you sound just like him," I say. "That is not living."

"You have to have faith that things can change. They've located the cluster of genes, and now the Rosetta Stone. Death doesn't have to be the only answer."

"Then what is? What do the other options look like? An existence like my mother's or your sister's? Is that living for you?"

He won't answer me. The repetitive screech of the wheel comes to a stop. I hear every sound acutely. Can smell the sour, musty odor of the animals. Feel the velvet of the yellow lights against my bare skin. I am here in the room and I am present. This is real. This is now. Rising from the couch, I hold my glass carefully out to Will.

"Thank you for the water." I wave at the animals. "And the company."

Will smiles and takes the glass from my hands. "I like coming here when I feel lost. Grace, you don't have to be alone with all this pain. I wish I had gotten to know your father better, but I do know he was so proud of you and loved you beyond this world."

"Sure," I say.

Will stands up beside me. "I want to help in whatever way I can. Let me help you."

"Thank you. I'm good now."

"Maybe you need a change of scenery. It's these long winters. How about a trip to the beach? Head to the ocean?"

"Is that your answer for everything?"

"Sun. Vitamin D." Will holds up his arms like he is being bathed in sunlight. "Yes, this doctor would say that is a cure-all."

I smirk at Will's conviction, but his expression makes

me feel the heat of the sun. The rays penetrating the layers of my skin. And then memory of a voice enters my mind. The feel of her hand cupping the round of my shoulder. *Don't fall asleep. You'll burn.*

"I wish it was that simple," I say, and walk away from Will, my footsteps deliberate and clear on the hard concrete floor. I open the door to a maze I no longer know how to maneuver.

WinterSpringSummer Autum

Her footsteps sounded so hollow in the empty house. Wandering from room to room, she called for her mother.

"Where are you?" she cried. Mama had left so suddenly from underneath the table. But after some time, when Mama did not return, she crawled out from under the table to find the kitchen empty.

She wandered upstairs, but the quiet bedrooms offered her no answers. Downstairs, the living room where her mother and father had just been, the disorderly pillows on the couch giving away the past, was now empty except for the swaying shadows on the carpet cast by the large maple tree outside in the neighbor's yard.

She went into the hallway and stared at the basement

door. Slowly she opened it and stood at the top, gazing down into the open black maw.

"Mama?"

The darkness mocked her, but she refused to step into the trap. "Mama?"

She closed the door.

Could her mother have left her alone in the house? Maybe she had gone to the grocery store. She began to think about her father. About calling him at work, even though she knew he would be busy. But Mama was gone. She made up her mind that this was what they called an emergency. Sometimes in an emergency, you had to disturb people.

She walked into the kitchen to study the list of emergency numbers that her mother had taped to the wall next to the phone. But before she could pick up the receiver, she saw a shoe. And then the other a few feet away. Her mother's empty shoes were on the floor, where they had not been earlier. Mama was back.

She stepped toward the kitchen table and saw a shadow moving underneath.

"Mama?" She slowly raised up the corner of the tablecloth. Huddled on the floor, knees to chin, her mother gazed up at her.

"Mama?"

Her mother's hand quickly jerked out, clasping her ankle. With a violent yank, she was back under the table. Mama held out a knife.

"We are not going to escape. We have to face the train. We have to do it together. You have to be brave. We are not going to let the train take us away."

Mama held the large kitchen knife straight up in the air; the whites of her knuckles gleamed while clenching the handle.

She stared at the sharp, shining blade and began to tremble.

Vinter Spring SummerAutumn

I shudder in terror as I make turn after turn in the hall-way. With each step, each corner, the planes of this world shuffle like playing cards. By the time I find the familiar centrifuge machine marked number four, I am ready to cry from pure relief. I grip the edge of the machine and gather my thoughts. I know where to go from here.

With my vision kaleidoscoping, I edge along the wall and open the door to a familiar lab room. I reach the assignment postings. The singular line of the clipboards hang one right next to the other. I count them over and over again, the repetition and order focusing me. Deep breaths. I know how to do this. I know what this means.

I find my name and draw my index finger along the

notes. Inventory duty today. With clipboard in hand, I head across the hall to the supply room. It's blissfully empty and quiet. The chemicals, solutions, lab ware, all twinkle at me from the organized shelves. Working my way down the row, notating what needs to be reordered, my heart returns to beating regularly and my vision remains singular and clear. Low on twelve-millimeter pipettes. Need more pH paper. No more stirring bars. I lift up a bottle of hydrochloric acid. Barely any there. I record all this in neat, precise letters.

As I search behind a group of half-gallon jugs, checking to see how much more I need to reorder, Dr. Mendelson's voice jumps into my mind. I replay her words. Did she really ask me to join her lab? The shadowy remnants of our conversation steal out of reach. The betrayal of my mind angers me, and a prickling along the skin of my scalp spreads to the edges of my earlobes. I reach up and pinch the flesh. Focus, I repeat silently. Focus. It doesn't matter. I can't let myself return to what I cannot know. I know how to take inventory. The work tames my mind.

I jot down the number four next to the hydrochloric acid on my list and check the reorder box. I walk down another row. Low on isopropyl alcohol. Barely any blue pH-10 buffer solution. The prickling returns, but this time it runs from my lobe all the way down the nape of my neck. Maybe I'm having an allergic reaction to the animals I was with earlier. I itch the back of my neck and return to the list.

"Death doesn't have to be the only answer," Will says.

Walking forward along the row, I check the bottles of nitric acid. Plenty.

"What is faith but blind hope?" Dr. Mendelson asks.

The prickling spreads down my shoulders. I focus on my steps, nice and easy, one foot in front of the other. Check the list. Sulfuric acid. Fine.

A distant faint grating of metal on metal. Just a cart passing in the hall, I reason with myself.

Potassium cyanide.

Unless . . .

I jump.

The burning sensation creeps down my back, and I set down the clipboard on the shelf. My entire body is aflame, and I claw at my shoulders and the sides of my head. My ears begin to pound with the noise of grinding iron.

It was her choice.

Take it.

It's right in front of you.

Take it.

I reach forward and take the potassium cyanide bottle. The silence descends so abruptly that I turn around in shock. When you live with noise all the time, the quiet can be disturbing. I grip the bottle tightly and shove it into my jeans pocket. Whipping off my lab coat and balling it up, I rush out the inventory room and into the interns' assignment room. I grab my backpack off the hooks and shove my lab coat on a shelf. I head to the elevators. Another intern rounds the corner and I wave.

"Can you tell Dr. Diaz I went for my dinner break?" I call. The elevator doors open and I step inside without hearing the answer. The doors close behind me.

The prickling is completely gone by the time I walk through the lobby and push open the glass doors to leave Genentium. Outside, it has become night. For once, I feel a warmth in the air. The lights from the diner beckon me and I remember the night I had to read Stephanie's name tag as though meeting her for the first time. I close my eyes on the memory. Dad and I had practically lived at the diner; Stephanie like a wife and mother, laughing at all our stupid lab jokes.

What do chemists use to make guacamole?

Avogadros.

I grip the bottle in my pocket, the grooved ridges of the top filling me with immeasurable relief, and a weightlessness buoys my body. The train cannot reach me now. The rumble of cars passing along the streets, the faint buzz of tungsten streetlamps, the voices of a couple talking as they walk by me, I can hear all of it. The world opens before my eyes. A ravenous hunger descends along with a feeling of joy with each pang. I know exactly who I am.

I push open the door to the diner and spot Stephanie at the far end of the counter. I wave to her and take my usual seat by the cash register.

"Hey, sweetheart." Stephanie walks over. "It's good to see you back."

"Hey, Steph. I'm sorry about the other night. I must have given you a scare."

Stephanie leans her elbows on the counter and hunches toward me. She whispers, "Gracie, I have never seen you look that way. Even right after your daddy died, you still had that spirit inside you. But the other night, I thought I was seeing your lost ghost walk in."

"I'm better," I say.

Stephanie leans in closer and meets my eyes. "I can see that." She straightens up and winks. "Will seems like a nice guy."

Immediately, a blush blooms on my cheeks and I wish I had my summer tan to hide my reaction. Stephanie grins, seeing my reaction.

"You want your usual?"

I nod.

Stephanie pushes open the swinging door to the kitchen and steps inside. A cloud of steam rises up from a pot on the stove. The soft white billow shifts and moves like a phantom before the door swings closed. I reach down into the pocket of my jeans and grip the bottle for relief. I grab a nearby newspaper and quickly scan the headlines to keep my mind preoccupied.

Stephanie returns after a few minutes and slides a plate loaded with mashed potatoes and meat loaf in front of me before moving over to a group ready to order. I sit up straighter on my stool and breathe in deeply the familiar aromas. It's been a long time since I've had real food. I cut into the tender meat with my fork and place it in my mouth. As I chew, a wave of nausea makes it hard to swallow. It must be from eating all the canned food. My body probably can't tolerate anything else. I grip the side of my plate and try a scoop of mashed potatoes. My stomach heaves. I stand up quickly and rush to the bathroom. After splashing water on my face, I stare at my clammy reflection in the mirror and will myself to keep it together. My mouth pools with saliva, and I clench my jaw hard against the rising bile, but it's too late. I turn around and vomit.

Winter Spring Summer Autumn

The sudden lurch of your stomach as though you have jumped from a cliff will awaken you. Your breath quickens as you sit up from your dreams, which will follow you into your waking world, the shrieks, the moaning and keening like a torture chamber of suffering. You will gaze around your room, knuckles to teeth, searching for the source, somebody in great pain.

The air will thicken with the reverberations. Every molecule ripe with anguish. You will feel as though your ears are bleeding from the cries, your throat scraped raw from the screams, your skin ripped open from the clawing.

You will crawl to the floor and hide under the bed, curling into a ball, your hands covering your ears, rocking back and forth, keeping time as you wait for the wails to stop.

The sound of pounding feet and the door being flung open will alarm you. Strong hands gripping your arms and dragging you out from underneath the bed. You will scream and flail, trying to escape their brutality as you bite and hit until they strap your wrists to the bed rails and cover your body with a net that presses you back firmly into the mattress like a swaddled baby. You will feel the sharp press of the needle piercing your skin.

Slowly, the familiar siren song of sleep will arrive. Their voices surrounding you as you sink back into yourself, back to the empty basement of dreams where a mother weeps for her child. You will close your eyes, wondering who they are.

Spring

A voice wakes me from my stupor on the floor next to the toilet.

"Grace." The knocking comes again. "Grace, are you okay?"

I will myself off the floor of the bathroom and stagger over to the sink to rinse out my mouth. "Be right out."

I examine myself in the mirror. Who will I become? I feel as though I am rotting from the inside out. A shell of a human being, the decay unperceivable until touched, and then I will disintegrate right on the spot.

Placing my palm over the reflection of my face, I suddenly long for my father. I desperately want the life he promised me when I was still that little girl and believed everything he said. I want oceans and pizza and play-grounds and snow and ice cream. You will live and die each day only to be reborn to repeat the cycle all over again. You will—

I smash my fist into the mirror. A spiderweb of splin-tered glass erupts.

The doorknob jiggles wildly. "GRACE! Come out right now or I'm gonna break down this door!"

I open the door.

Stephanie's face, marbled with worry, meets mine.

"I'm okay."

Stephanie steps back and then checks me over from head to toe, studying my body and face for clues.

"I'm sorry about the mirror. I'll pay for it," I say, and try to move past her.

She grabs my arms. "You scared the shit out of me. What is going on, Grace?"

"Nothing," I say.

"Smashing a mirror is not nothing," Stephanie insists.

"I'm going to be late for work. Just leave it, okay? I'm fine, Stephanie." Irritation husks my voice.

Stephanie squints at me, steps back, and gives me a thorough exam. She licks her lips as though she is about to lay into me, but instead she sighs and turns. "I'll pack your dinner to go."

I glance back at the broken mirror and then follow her to the counter.

Stephanie quickly boxes up my cold, untouched dinner and puts it in a bag. She holds it out and I reach over to take it from her.

"You have to eat all of it, you hear me?" Stephanie says.

I nod, but I can't meet her eyes.

"Gracie," she says, and waits for me to look up. "You know I am here for you, honey. If you need someone to talk to, I can help you with that. You can't do this by yourself. You are not alone. Please, let me help you through this."

I see the concern in her eyes and remember all those dinners when she would laugh with me and Dad. Shaking her head at his bad jokes. Without thinking, I reach out and grip her forearm. "Thank you for everything, Stephanie. You've been a real friend, and I am never going to forget that."

Stephanie squirms for a second in embarrassment. "Yeah, well, just don't forget to come pay your tab plus one broken mirror at the end of the month."

I refuse to make empty promises, so I smile instead.

She pours a new hot coffee into a paper cup and seals on the lid before handing it over to me.

I hoist my backpack onto one shoulder and with coffee and dinner in hand, I turn slightly to push open the door with my shoulder. Behind me the diner is warm with heat and food, chatter and clanking dishes. Stephanie stands in her place, watching me, then waves before turning to another customer, pulling out her pen and pad. My heart aches when I think about Stephanie finding out what will happen to me. But these are things I cannot control, and Stephanie's pain is another drop in a pool teeming with heartache.

Outside, I stare up at the Genentium sign but head toward my car. I cannot wait any longer. I had thought having made my choice would have kept the train at bay for a little longer, but after the incident in the bathroom, I know I have to act now.

Across the street, Will stands and waves his arms high in the air as though flagging down an ambulance. When I don't cross over to him but keep heading down the sidewalk toward the parking lot, he dashes across the street.

"Hey, didn't you see me?"

"How could I miss you?" I ask. "I'm not feeling so hot, so I'm just gonna head home."

"No, you can't!" Will says, and reaches for my elbow, making the coffee slosh out of the small hole in the container and burning my hand.

"Oww, Jesus!"

"No, it's Will." He points to himself.

"Oh my God, you are maddening," I say, but can't help smiling. I continue walking toward the parking lot. Will keeps in step next to me.

"Are you following me?"

"Yes, I am," Will says, as though it is the most normal thing in the world.

"I told you I'm going home." The annoyance makes my voice high.

"But I want to show you something."

"Now?" I show him my box of dinner. "Can't it wait until tomorrow?"

"Come on. You can leave that in your car. It'll take one second, and you are going to be blown away. I promise."

I consider the bottle in my lab coat. The weight of it pulling gently on the pocket. The insurance makes me bold with my time. I still have tonight. "Okay."

He smiles broadly and jabs his thumb to the right. We walk quickly to my car and I dump my already cold dinner and coffee on my seat with my backpack. Will touches my elbows and hurries ahead of me, waving at me to hurry too. We practically run past the lab toward a part of the city I have never explored. After a few blocks I feel my blood warming from our fast pace.

"So you're not going to tell me the surprise?"

"Nope."

"Not even a hint?"

"Nope."

"God, what kind of scientist are you? At least tease me with a formula."

Will starts laughing. "You are such a nerd."

"Hey, don't blame me. Dad created an actual formula for perfect cheese on toast when I got mad at him one too many times for forgetting to pick up the pizza. I have the equation up on the fridge."

"Actually, he showed me that formula. It was ingenious. The bread-to-cheese ratio divided by time. He even had the width of the toast slice down to the millimeter."

"See what I had to deal with all that time?"

Will turns to look at me, and the glow of the sunset brushes his face. He is summer gold, warmth and light. I halt midstep in surprise. I know Will. The feeling of familiarity like he has always been beside me, walking with me, talking with me, gazing at me. How long have I known him? Why can't I remember? Nothing rational can explain the feeling that we have met before.

Will takes my hand as we cross another street, and he gently pulls me across an abandoned parking lot pockmarked and claimed by weeds. A chain-link fence at the far end stops our journey.

"Damn, I thought we would be able to get past these buildings," Will says.

"This is what you wanted to show me?" I ask, looking around.

"No, look between the two buildings," Will instructs.

I gaze out and see the edge of the river and the lowering sun reflecting off the water. The view is so narrow it's hard to say that it's beautiful. I don't want to disappoint Will, so I continue to just stare out at the water as though it is something magnificent to behold.

A faint tremor livens the ground. I clutch the chain-link fence. The vibrations echo through the metal. The distant shriek of a whistle squirms into my ears. The train. I hear the train coming. I feel myself tense, ready to run. I can outrun it. I reach into my coat pocket and grip the bottle. I will not let it take me.

I turn quickly on my heels.

"Grace, please, just wait," he says.

The ground is shaking. The rhythmic clank of the wheels against iron tracks. The steady blare of the horn. I have to leave now. The train cannot take me. I know I will not come back this time.

"Let me go, Will. I have to leave."

"But you're going to miss it."

The low, haunting, rhythmic grind of metal against metal. The ringing bell and screaming whistle barrel into me. I hold my hands over my ears.

Will points and I follow his hand, glimpsing between the buildings, blocking the view of the river, the moving train. I lower my hands and grip the fence, pressing my forehead to the cold wire.

"It's the five-ten freight train," Will shouts into the noise.

I automatically begin to count the cars the way I used to do when I was so young. The sound of the passing train, an external heartbeat clear and proud, lulls me just like before. The whistle blows and the crisp, deep timbre echoes through my body, a beacon of truth and dignity. The ghost of what I have been hearing and living with in my mind is nothing like the reality of the strength that reverberates out from the passing cars. A final whistle blow and the last car disappears from sight. I close my eyes, relishing the fading rumble. Then silence.

Will cups the roundness of my shoulder. Light, but reassuring. I turn to him in gratefulness and surprise.

"You said you heard a train, so I started asking around," Will says, still gazing out between the buildings as though watching the phantom train. "I don't know how you could have heard it from down below in the lab, but maybe you have some extrasensory auditory powers."

"All this time that I've been working at Genentium I've never heard it pass before," I say. "I don't understand how I could have missed it."

"If you were down in the lab every night around this time, you wouldn't know it existed. There's only one train every week or so. It's an old track. Most of the trains use the newer one on the other side of the city."

"And you just happened to catch me at the diner just as this train was about to pass?"

"Well, I am a researcher, you know. I looked up the schedule, but catching you at the diner, that was luck. Or fate."

"You sound like Dr. Mendelson."

"Maybe there is a reason she's a genius."

"Funny." I start to walk away.

"Wait, Grace. Can I have your phone for a second?"

"No."

"Please, just for a second. I forgot mine at the lab."

He is getting me to do all kinds of things tonight. I pull out my phone from my back pocket and hand it over. He quickly types something and then hands it back.

"That's it? That's all you had to do?"

"Yup. Now you have my number."

I look down at my phone and see that I am calling someone. Will. "And you have my number," I say.

"That's how it works," he says lightly, and turns to leave.

I turn around one last time and gaze down the narrow alley between the buildings that just a minute ago proved that I was not crazy.

All this time could I really have been hearing a real train when I thought I was imagining things? Can I rule this out as a possibility? I slip my hand into the sleeve of my other arm, dig my nails in hard. The pain feels real.

WinterSpringSummer Autum

She balled her hands into fists and dug her nails deep into the palms of her hands. She repeated to herself that she could not cry. Mama did not like when she cried.

The knife blade, long and straight, caught a glint of sunlight and refracted the light. What did Mama want to do with the knife? How was it going to stop the train? She did not understand. She did not want to understand.

"Mama, I want to call Daddy," she whispered.

"Shhhh," Mama said, her face calm and relaxed now that she clutched a knife. A yawn spread her mouth wide and open. The darkness and pearl points of teeth. "I am so tired." Mama said. "Let me rest."

"Let's go lie down, Mama. Let's take a nap." The blank expression on Mama's face unnerved her.

"We will rest and never have to worry about the train again," Mama said.

The words Mama spoke stilled her heart.

Mama moved the knife to one hand and with the other hand, reached out to her. "Come here." Mama pulled her close and then placed the blade against the pillowed fat of her cheekbone. The ridge and edge forming an indented line. A line long as a road on a winter barren night.

Winter **Spring** SummerAutum

The darkness surrounds me as I drive home. My lone pair of headlights are the only ones on the dirt road so far from everything. The feeling of safety has left with Will after he dropped me off at the parking lot and returned to the lab. Seeing the train has made my mind fragile, swirling with the reality of what this new truth means. The train is real. The train is real. Could I have been hearing a real distant train from the house? I've searched online for rail routes, but maybe there was an old track that was only used once in a while near the house as well? If so, then what did it mean? I wasn't imagining things at home? The train could be real?

All that I thought I knew tilts off-kilter. As I drive, slowly navigating around the ruts and potholes left over in the road from the thaw of spring, I track the possibilities. What is inevitable? Predictable? And all the permutations in between. Do I dare hope? I place my hand over the bottle in my pocket. What was so certain is now fading into haze like the condensing fog before me. My headlights illuminate ghostly wisps of vapor on large swaths of brown fields, the snow finally almost gone. The last tentacles of winter releasing their grip.

Ahead of me, I see my house emerging from the patches of snow and field. Soon the forget-me-nots will come into bloom. As much as I complained to Dad about being in the middle of nowhere, I was looking forward to seeing the periwinkle clusters all around the house like the way it looked when we first visited a year ago. There was a melancholy sweetness to seeing their abundance, which Dad had taken for a sign. The flowers foretelling all that was to come, while I saw them as a reminder of all that had passed. Mom could still be out there. I might have a chance at not being an orphan. If I let myself search the way Dad did, could the risk pay off? My heart beats wildly. The gamble of learning the truth thrums through my veins. If hope is the thing with feathers that perches in the soul, as Emily Dickenson believed, then maybe that explains this flutter in my body.

The house is dark as I draw closer. Not a single light. Not even a light on the porch above the front door. I always forget to turn it on before I leave in the mornings. For someone who is always considering genetic changes for the future, I definitely don't know how to plan for the future in a single day. The bleakness of the house confronts me in a way I never realized before. There is no warm, welcoming feel. It stands there so lonely and still, a shadowy reminder of all that I have lost. Alone, wandering through the empty rooms, most of which have no furniture because it was always just Dad and me. A cloak of sadness like a black shawl curves over my shoulders, and I hunch forward in dread of the empty, lonely night. I have to remember the porch light tomorrow. Tomorrow, I marvel to myself. There is a tomorrow?

As I pull into the driveway, a dark form moves on the porch. My heart lurches in surprise and fear. I cover my face with my hands and count to five and then slowly lower them. A figure stands in the headlights of my car, staring at me through the windshield.

"Hannah?"

I quickly cut the engine, kill the lights, and open the door.

"What happened? Are you okay?"

It is hard to see her in the darkness. Remembering my box of food, I lean back into the car and pull it out along with the coffee.

"Did you eat? I have some dinner. We can share." I chuckle. "Forget it, I don't want my hand anywhere near your mouth when you're eating. I'll just have my coffee and some soup."

Hannah nods, but still won't speak.

I lead her into the house. A sudden freezing blast of wind blows the door in just as I open it. I realize once we step into the hallway that Hannah has never been over to my house before. Not even after my father died. I shut the door and turn on the lights. Hannah's haggard face swims in front of mine. I am overwhelmed by a feeling of displacement for a second, and then the house revolves back into position. Focusing on keeping my balance, I head toward the kitchen to warm up the food.

"Come on," I call. "It's meat loaf."

Hannah follows me, but then stops at the doorway of the kitchen. I wave at the table, but she remains standing. As I place the box of food into the microwave above the stove, the bottle in my front pocket jams into my thigh as I lean against the counter. I take it out, setting it down next to the cold coffee.

"Grace, I'm scared."

I turn around. I know this fear as though it were on my own face.

"What are we supposed to do?" She places her hands on her stomach. "Who am I to think I can be a mother?"

"What happened, Hannah?"

"I can't give her the life she should have."

"You have to think about what's best for your life, too, Hannah."

"My life, Grace?"

"Yes. Yours. We all have choices. Things might seem crazy and impossible." I can feel Will's hands on my shoulder as we watched the train pass. "But it doesn't have to be that way," I say. "Maybe more things are possible than we realize."

Hannah gazes down at her hands cradling the slight bulge pushing forward. The microwave beeps, startling me. "Come on. You look like you could use some meat loaf. It's from the diner." I reach into the microwave and take out the cardboard container, set it down on the counter.

"What is that?" Hannah points at the brown bottle next to the cup of coffee.

I glance over at the potassium cyanide. "That's a choice that I thought I had to make." Reaching up into the cabinet, I take out a plate and begin to transfer the meat loaf from the container.

"It's not a choice." Dad walks into the kitchen past Hannah and moves over to the sink. He crosses his arms.

"She can make her own decisions," Hannah says.

I look up from the plate and glance over at Dad. In the reflection of the window above the sink, I find myself standing alone in the kitchen. A faint whistle echoes in the distance. Hannah heard Dad. One knee buckles, and I shift my eyes between them. Hannah heard Dad. My breath catches in my throat. This is not possible. Hannah and Dad watch each other. A high-pitched noise, the grinding of metal on metal, worms into my ears. No, no, no. The train is real. I saw it today. It's real. It is real.

"Grace." Dad steps over to me. "Grace, I know you can do this. Push back against the sounds. They are not real."

Hannah takes one step into the kitchen. "Are you real?"

Dad points at Hannah. "STOP!"

"I won't let you do this to her," Hannah says.

"I'm trying to save her, just like I tried to save you." Dad pleads, "Please, please give her a chance."

"You didn't save me!" Hannah shouts.

"I TRIED!" Dad yells back.

There is a faint trembling rising up from my feet. A clear, sharp whistle pierces lightly, then disappears. I reach over and grip the brown bottle. "LEAVE ME ALONE!" I scream.

"Grace, this isn't you," Dad begs.

"Dad, what's going on?"

Hannah takes another step into the kitchen. "She knows what's coming for her. She can make her own choice to stop it."

I stare at her face. The gentle bow of her upper lip. The pink labyrinth swirls of her ears. The blade line of her jaw. This face I know in my heart before I can remember her name. I know how she likes to blow her bangs off her forehead when she is tired. How her eyes squint crescent moons when she laughs. Her voice reading to me at night. I have missed her so much. My mother. She came back for me when I needed her the most. Standing beside me, my mother and father, as it was always supposed to be, and yet I do not gaze up into the reflection of us in the window above the sink. For I know from the outside what a stranger would see passing by this house alone in its field of forget-me-nots.

"No, no, no." Dad shakes his head, his voice trembling.

"Hannah, you must leave her alone. She has a chance to get better."

"Don't you get it?" Hannah says, taking another step forward. "You want her to rot in some hospital waiting for a miracle. Do you really want her to live scared and drugged out of her mind? That's the kind of life you want for our daughter?"

Dad holds out his hands. "Grace, listen to me. Please. Concentrate on my words. Block out everything else. Listen to me, Grace. Things can change. There are new developments all the time. You have to have faith."

A sudden vibration almost sways me off balance. A growing thunder thrums in my ears. The clatter of tracks rattles hard against my heart. There is no more time. The train was not real. I cannot trust myself. I have to do this quickly before I fall. My hands are shaking so hard I can barely get the lid off the coffee cup. Half of it spills on the counter. I twist open the cap of the bottle and start to pour the white crystalline grains into the coffee.

"NO, GRACE!" Dad shouts in my ears, and I drop the bottle on the floor. The white crystals spill everywhere. Dad's voice clings to me. "I know I wasn't there for you in all the ways you needed. I was doing my best for us as a family. But it was always all for you. I love you, Grace. Please don't do this."

"You left me," I cry. "You were never around for me. You were always trying to find her . . . find a cure for her!" I point at Hannah.

"No, bugaboo. There was such little time left after we

moved here. I had to do everything in my power to help you before the illness got worse. Bug, I was doing it all for you. *You.* You are my life."

I see his face so clearly. Drop by drop, all the sadness of what has never been said, the words trail down the worn grooves of his face. Those horizon-blue eyes begging me to stay with him. He fought until his last breath. For me? For me.

"Daddy . . . Help me."

His eyes squint in pain and he bows his head, unable to bear my words. I know if he could, he would make the sun orbit the earth, make the waves crash against the horizon, unravel a miracle from a strand of DNA. The train thunders closer. I push my fingers through my hair and pull hard against the roots. I need to feel something to keep my mind present. My nails claw into my forearm and vermillion specks rise to the surface of my skin. This is real. This is now. Isn't it?

Dad watches me tear at myself to stay present and his eyes fill with tears. "Grace, there will be new advances. There will be more they can do. You have to keep fighting. Keep faith."

Hannah takes another step and faces me. We are the same height. We have the same hair. We have the same angel's-kiss birthmark on the side of our neck.

A trilling sound floats into the air.

"Answer it, Grace," Dad says. "It's Will. Let him help you."

"Just like Dave?" Hannah says. "He said he loved her."

"You said you loved us!" Dad argues. "And you left."

Hannah's face crumples as though he has punched her. "I did what I thought was best for you and Grace. It was the hardest decision I ever made. But it was my choice." Hannah looks at the coffee cup. "This is a choice."

"That is not an option." Dad walks up behind me.

I stand between my parents. Caught in their love for each other and for me. The beat of the train tracks drums into my veins. The heavy clanking grows louder and louder. I lift the coffee cup from the counter. Inside this murky darkness is my truth. Hannah steps even closer until our noses are almost touching. The shadows creep into the corners of my eyes.

"Drink it now. The train is coming. Your life will not be yours. You will always be at the mercy of the disease and the drugs."

The faint trilling fills the air again.

"Will knows what to do. Trust him," Dad says.

The train whistle slices through my mind and I grimace as I absorb the pain. I must do this now if I want to keep the train from taking me, and I can no longer control my thoughts or my actions.

"No, Grace," Dad cries. "Please, bug. Put down the cup. Call Will. Do this for me."

The clanking sound of wheels against tracks grows louder, unrelenting as sliver by sliver I begin to dissolve. It takes every ounce of concentration to move my unsteady hand, inch by inch, raising the cup to my lips. A bead of sweat slides down the side of my face. I see the cliff's edge drawing nearer. I must jump or I will fall.

"Daddy, I can't live this way. I don't want to live this way. Forgive me."

I tip back the cup, but my quivering hand sloshes the liquid down the front of my shirt. It burns sharp, the etching rawness silencing the train for a moment, and I tear away the fabric from the skin of my stomach. And there. There. The evidence. There is a taut swelling. A soft curve pushing forward. I gasp and raise my eyes to Hannah's. All the seasons of her life in those eyes.

"Mama."

Her form fades slowly like mist in sunlight.

I set the cup back down on the counter and rip off my shirt. Pulling the phone from my back pocket, I call Will, but before I can speak, the shrieking howl of the whistle strikes me, lances through me.

The train explodes my mind. The skittering insects crawl inside and out, over my body, and I scream, tearing, ripping, scratching at them. Worthless. Disgusting. The Moirai. Come to me. Clotho. Lachesis. Atropos. Playing god now, are you? No. Yes. Stop.

I fail.

I fall.

Fall.

Forward.

Over the bridge.

Spring slips into summer.

Summer smolders down for autumn.

Autumn kneels to winter.

Winter yields. Spring.

Spring Slips into Summer

I watch the seasons pass from the window of a large cavernous room filled with other bodies. Hear the click of the clock's hand turning and turning. Time moves forward, but all I know is that the present becomes past. The future has become my reality. And the past, the past, a history that will repeat itself, clone itself, coded into the genomes of our lives, living and waiting to be birthed into the future.

I take my pills when I am told to. I sleep when I am told to. I eat when I am told to. And when no one is telling me what to do, I claw the walls for answers. Where is my name? I search every day to find my name. I know it is hidden behind the walls. I try to carefully tear apart the seams when no one is watching.

There are no more straps on my bed. The nurses smile and say I am making progress. The doctors nod. Nine pills become eight. Eight become seven. Seven become six. But still, I cannot find my name.

If I press my ears to the walls, I hear the faintest call from the other side. I know my name lives beyond what I can see.

Until one day, as I am walking by the television room, I hear a voice.

"Ma–ma."

I run to the sound. A child moves in the square of the picture.

The soft, wet, gurgling coos come back. "Ma–ma."

My name. My name. Out from the walls. Into my ears. Inside my body. I claim it. I clutch it like a lifeline. Hand over hand I struggle to stop the moving train. It slows. The whistle quiets. I listen again. "Mama."

The white light above my head beats into my skull as I sit in a line with all the others. The nurse goes down the row. She hands out the pills and small cups of water. Some will swallow them quickly and leave. Others sit staring down into the delicate white cups like muffin tin papers meant for sweet things, not these bitter soothsayers.

I stare at the colored pebbles in my muffin cup and count them in my head. One two three four five six. Six. How many were there last time? Why can't I remember? The pills rob my mind. I think about throwing them like someone down the line has done, but then the bigger nurses jump up. My body remembers what happens next.

How many pills are there? I count them again. And then once more. One two three four five six. And somewhere in the counting, her face bubbles up. Then the scent of her hair like earth after a good rain. The memory of her stills the echoing chamber of my mind. I try and hold on to it, hold it so hard the paper cup of water crumples in my hand and the wetness coats my skin, soaks into the cotton of my pants. Her name tingles the tip of my tongue. But one of the stronger nurses watches me and starts to stand as she sees the puddle of water on the floor. I take the pills dry, placing each one at the back of my tongue and gathering saliva in my mouth. As each one slides down my throat, I realize the memory of her will fade with each swallow. . . . So I fold her essence deep down like lost hieroglyphics waiting to be unearthed.

Summer Smolders Down
for Autumn

You will bury your nose in the top of her head. The smell of her hair. You will remember it reminds you of the air after the rains, of earth cleansed and reborn. The weight of her delicate fairy bones against yours. The gentle plane of her neck gliding down into the rounding curve of her shoulder. Her life will press against your chest, into your heart, entwining your beats until they are one. This child of grace and beauty. And all that had been lost will rush back. You will feel yourself a hurricane bearing down on the tender souls meant for fair weather.

She will press against you. Her thin arms haloing your neck.

And the faint exhale of her breath will overtake the

roar of the train. You will drop the knife to the floor as the sobs rack your body. And as you sink your face into her neck, in that moment, the smell of her childhood will fill you with wonder and dread. How has all this come to pass? You will wonder at the ceaseless cycles like the seasons, the press of life stampeding, thundering, coming for you over and over again. You will wonder when it will ever end. The knife blade glints sharp with clarity. You will kick it away and grab her, emerging from under the table.

She doesn't move from your side but stares up. Watching and waiting. You know you have to call him. Tell him what has happened. You know what is to come next. You know from what has been lived before. And before that. And before that. Each time winter falls, there is only the hope for spring and by the grace of love, you will return to them again. But for now, for now, you will walk away to save them. To save her.

Her endless counting. Of train cars, weather, muffin papers, the hours, days, and months. Her wise eyes looking for you, into you. The you inside you inside you. She will wait patiently each time.

But before you move to begin what has already been, you will hold her one more time ever so tightly. Kneeling down on both knees so that you may fully embrace her. Worship at the altar of all that is whole and true and real. You will worship this child as your father and mother worshipped you. And you will know faith. And religion. And science. And hope. You will know what it means to believe. A singular belief that pierces more true than the ever-racing train across the landscape of your mind.

You will kiss her again as you slip her arms from your neck. Stand up and move to pick up your purse. Carefully, without turning around, you will open the door. Pause. Count each year of her life. And then you will step forward and walk into the days, months, years, seasons. To a place between breaths.

Autumn Kneels to Winter

She opened her eyes and sat up in bed. A searing pain tore through the lower half of her body, making her whimper and cry. Had it all been a dream then?

Is this how it ends?

No.

Would it be so awful if it did?

No.

The cycle broken.

No.

She gazed down and then slowly encircled her arms around her empty body. A man sat in a chair next to her bed. He leaned forward, his sky blue eyes wide and open with concern.

She gazed at him and tried to speak, but no words would come. The distant sound of a train moving toward her forced her eyes around the room.

He stood up and came to her, reaching out to take her hand. She shrank away. His face was so familiar. But strange. She could not remember, but felt in her heart that he was someone kind. He raised her hand and placed her palm on his cheek and held it there.

He slowly withdrew his hand and smiled gently when she did not remove hers from his face.

The train whistle blew long and hard. Her head turned wildly. Where was it? She needed to see it.

Keep fighting, bugaboo.

Why fight when the battle has been lost?

The train rattled closer, rumbling louder in her mind. She wanted to count the cars. Watch them move past. Feel the wind of their passing speed on her face like she had so long ago.

The man returned, holding a blanketed bundle. He sat down on the edge of her bed and lowered the bundle to her eyes.

"She is so beautiful, Grace."

Take it away. It should die. Death will save her. Kill it.

This child deserves every chance.

The translucent pink of her head poked out from the blanket.

Look at her. She is life itself.

Kill it.

The small pink face, eyes shut tight, the rash bump of a nose.

She will be just like us. She will suffer the same way.

No, there is a chance it will be different. The discovery of the gene . . .

The smell of milk and flowers. Forget-me-nots. She carefully reached out one finger. As she focused on the face and touched her finger three times to the child's fore-head, the silence in the room exploded into her mind. She gasped, "Hannah."

The man stared into her face. "Your mother's name? I'm going to make sure she's okay, Grace. I promise. She is going to wait for you. We are going to wait for you. Come back, Grace. Come back."

The distant rumbling returned and the familiar vibra-tions of the track soothed her pain. She closed her eyes. All that she had seen lost to blackness.

Death would stop the suffering.

Death is not an answer.

All you care about is a cure. Stop your madness. Kill the child. Save her from herself. Death. Death is a choice.

And so is life. The strength to believe and live. That is a choice.

This is not a real life.

She was on the train, moving moving away toward something nothing someone no one leaving returning sit-ting standing sleeping waking watching waiting.

Waiting.

Waiting waiting waiting waiting waiting waiting waiting waiting waiting in the place between breaths.

Winter Yields, Spring

We see you standing on a bridge, looking back at the life you have lived. The memories like clouds passing over the landscape of your face. The anguish that can only come from knowing how much you have loved and been loved. And to know you are losing that time. Forever.

We watch you hear what is coming forward across that bridge to you. The endless shrieks of a life that you do not want but cannot change. Like the Fates. They were never minor gods to you.

We see you standing on this bridge, fanning the cards of decision, the paths beaming out like endless rays into the future, the possibilities a forget-me-not flower seen from the eyes of a bee.

You know how to end your life.
Hers could be another story.
We cannot help you with this decision.
Yet when all is sifted, what remains?
Faith.